MIST ACROSS THE HILLS

by

JEAN S. MACLEOD

HARLEQUIN BOOKS

Winnipeg • Canada   New York • New York

MIST ACROSS THE HILLS

Originally published by Mills & Boon Limited,
50 Grafton Way, Fitzroy Square, London, England.

Harlequin edition published March, 1967
2nd U.S. Printing..........................May, 1967

FOR
JEAN DUNCAN

*All the characters in this book have no existence outside the
imagination of the Author, and have no relation whatsoever to
anyone bearing the same name or names. They are not even
distantly inspired by any individual known or unknown to the
Author, and all the incidents are pure invention.*

CHAPTER ONE

LOCH SOLAN

PERHAPS it had been foolish of her to come so far, Arline Hamilton reflected, as she gripped the tiller hard in her slim, brown hand, and turned to survey the rapidly blurring coastline beyond her small craft's wake. Perhaps it had been more stupid still to bring the boat out at all and venture across the loch alone for the first time in her life. She had handled the little craft often enough when her young cousin had been there to give her the confidence of his expert knowledge, but Douglas had always taken the tiller when they left the calmer waters of the bay behind and skimmed out into the Firth.

Theirs was the companionship of complete understanding, and Arline often wondered what life in the Penner household would have been like for her without the green oasis of her young cousin's friendship to turn to in the desert of her relations' bare tolerance.

It was hard enough to be an unwanted dependent, but harder still to realise that your efforts at independence were seldom recognised as such.

It had not been easy for Arline to promise her father that, on his death, she would seek out her mother's only brother, for easy-going Joel Hamilton had left his daughter very little of material value with which to face the world. Arline had managed her father's affairs for the year between her leaving school and his death, but twelve months had been too short a space of time to right the havoc wrought by years of indifference and a generosity that had been so frequently imposed upon.

Money had meant nothing to Joel Hamilton, and it meant very little to his daughter, but she recognised that, without it, she must learn to curb that fiercely independent spirit of hers which threatened every now and then to flame up and denounce the treatment meted out to her by her aunt, and, in a lesser degree, by her uncle.

It was this trouble that had brought her out across the waters of Loch Solan, with the rope twisted securely round her hand and the lug-sail billowing in the rising wind. It had been almost impossible to bite her even white teeth into her lower lip and keep silent before her aunt's tirade over a trifling mistake which had happened earlier in the day, and only her inherent love of keeping the peace had made Arline murmur an apology and seek the solitude of the shore as soon as her aunt had retired behind the banged door of her bedroom for her customary afternoon nap.

Arline had sought Douglas in vain, and had wandered down to the boat-house and unfastened the painter of the boat on the spur of the moment. Hoisting the sail with no little difficulty, she had found the wind in her favour, but though the fresh breeze from the hills cooled her hot cheeks, her thoughts still dwelt on the episode in the dining-room of "Braeside," and her aunt's sharp tongue still echoed in her ears.

How much longer would she be able to stand it, she wondered. She thought that she was repaying them in some small measure by her secretarial duties for the family in general, but recently even that had seemed to be considered an inadequate return for her keep.

When she realised that the bright sunshine of an hour back had dimmed to a hazy glow behind a thin and ominous-looking mist, she turned with a quick intake of breath to find that she had left the bay behind her and was far beyond Solan Point. She glanced at the sky, and the veiled sun and racing clouds sent a first quiver of apprehension through her.

She must turn back.

As if the elements had decided to vent their fury full upon her, the wind lashed against the sail and almost tore the helm from her fingers. She clung to it valiantly, and put all her remaining strength into another effort.

The boat responded, swerving round slowly but surely as it climbed out of the hollow of a wave and rode the crest of the next. With a little gasp of satisfaction Arline prepared to slide round the seat and let the big brown sail cross with the wind, but as she clung to the tiller with one hand and the rope cut into her other, a second fierce gust drove down the Firth, tearing the rope from her grasp. She clutched out wildly, catching it again, but with a crack of rending wood, the yard quivered and, doubling

4

into two broken spars, hung down against the flapping sail.

It was several seconds before Arline could fully realise what had happened, for with supreme presence of mind she had clung to the tiller and, using all her remaining strength, had saved her craft from being completely over-turned. The wind had whirled her round again, and she saw that she was drifting outwards, away from the bay and the friendly hills that swept down to the Point—drifting away towards the open Firth.

Panic seized her then, and for a moment she looked out helplessly at the grey, unfriendly sea about her, and saw no end to this catastrophe but the inevitable one of being swamped beneath those angry waters.

The need for action drove fear from her mind, giving her the calm courage which alone could pull her out of immediate danger. The sun had disappeared behind a mass of angry-looking cloud, and the sea had taken on the hue of lead. Away to the north she could see the dim outline of Mull shrouded in a veil of mist, and before her lay the grey expanse of the Firth of Lorne. She knew her danger, the danger of the innumerable little rocky islands that dotted the surface of the water—the islands that she had thought so beautiful and romantic as they lay under a bright sun.

The whine of the wind was in her ears now, and her eyes were strained to catch the first sign of water breaking in a white line on a rocky shore. If she were driven on to an island her frail boat would be completely wrecked.

For the first time she thought of the owner of the boat, and what her uncle would have to say about its loss should she ever reach "Braeside" again in safety. In her present predicament even "Braeside" seemed a desired haven. She thought of her cousin, and wished wholeheartedly that she had stayed to find him before setting out on this wild adventure.

Involuntarily she quivered. What could she do? Was there no way out of this dreadful situation? Her eyes sought the distant coastline which was all but lost to sight in the haze which swept down the Firth. Before her, the outline of a small island rose from the grey sea, and her heart thumped against her breast as she put all her energy into steering the boat past the jutting rocks.

Then, quite suddenly, across the water came the unmistakable sound of an engine. Arline sat up in her seat and turned in the direction of the sound. For a moment she could see nothing save the curtain of mist hanging down between her and the shore. I've been mistaken, she thought wildly, and the hope which had kindled within her at that first sound made her returning despair the deeper.

Once again, however, the sound came across the water, more steady now, as if the boat were drawing gradually nearer. Arline strained her eyes while she tried to arrest the mad career of her own craft. The sound of the engine behind her came nearer, and slowly out of the mist there appeared the white bow of a motor launch.

At that first, welcome sight Arline's tensed muscles relaxed, and she bent her head on her hands which still grasped the tiller. The realisation of all that might have happened seemed to sweep over her like an engulfing wave, carrying her forward on a rush of mingled fear and relief. When she lifted her head at last, the white launch was only a few yards behind her.

It was a small boat, little bigger than her own disabled craft, but to Arline the beat of its engine was as the trickle of running water is to a wanderer in an arid land. It was release from fear; it was help—life itself.

As the launch came nearer, she noticed that behind the green canvas awning a man stood watching her. He was the sole occupant of the oncoming craft, and he bent occasionally to the engine as he manœuvred the launch up to the drifting boat. He spoke across the water at last, and his voice was gruff and almost unfriendly:

"Keep her nose to the wind and sit still where you are."

Arline grasped the tiller firmly and obeyed him automatically. She could not bring herself to speak and, somehow, she felt that speech was about the most unnecessary thing at the moment. The stranger's whole attitude inferred that, as he bent to the engine and then stood up, with a long boat-hook in his hand.

"Hold on to your tiller, and when I say the word—jump!" he commanded, as he drew the two boats inch by inch together.

Arline felt her knees beginning to tremble, but she braced herself for the effort, realising subconsciously that she must

6

not fail him. Her eyes were on the white side of the launch as the grey lane of water between the two boats narrowed and for a moment the thought of the depths which lay beneath her turned her heart sick within her.

"Now!"

The curt command banished all thoughts from her mind save the need for immediate action. She rose unsteadily to her feet, grasping her own tiller to the last moment, and then, with a tremendous effort, she leapt the distance from one boat to the other.

Stumbling forward, she almost fell into the engine-well of the launch, but a firm brown hand grasped her arm and steadied her as she sank down on the cushions of the nearest seat.

It was a full minute before she could lift her eyes to the man who had come to her aid so timely. When she did so, she found that his back was turned towards her and that he was grappling for her disabled craft with the boat-hook.

"Can I—help?" she asked, realising that her voice was hoarse and shaking.

"No—sit where you are."

He had spoken without turning, and a little chill went through Arline as she noted the displeasure in the deep voice. Of course, he must consider her a complete fool, she supposed, and the thought increased her confusion. Her eyes rested on his broad back where his muscles showed through the grey sweater with the exertion of his efforts to bring her boat alongside.

He straightened at last and turned to her.

"I'm afraid we'll have to let her go," he said.

"It doesn't matter. Don't—don't bother," Arline murmured, aware that his grey eyes were upon her, and feeling more confused than ever under his cool stare.

He shrugged imperceptibly.

"It seems a shame to let a decent little craft like that go," he said. "She'll probably smash herself to pieces on one of those treacherous islands further down the Firth."

It seemed to Arline that his concern was more for her boat than for her own safety at the moment. When he looked at her his expression was stern, his mouth grim.

7

Yet, the rush of relief at her rescue overcame her momentary confusion.

"I—how can I thank you for what you have done?" she began hesitatingly, but he broke in with a brief laugh that was hardly mirthful.

"Don't begin to thank me until I've landed you safely on shore again," he said.

His manner implies that I should never have left the shore in the first place, Arline thought, and was surprised at the stirring anger within her. Why should he speak to her like this? She hadn't asked him to rush to her rescue. The ungraciousness of the thought pulled her up. He had every reason to be angry, she supposed. She glanced up at him.

The engine was chugging noisily again, and he turned the launch to go back the way he had come. With one firm, brown hand grasping the tiller, he was studying her closely. His expression was still grim, but his stern mouth had relaxed a little.

"What in heaven's name tempted you to come so far?" he asked at last.

"I—I had no idea that I had come so far," she defended herself weakly. "I wasn't thinking about—the boat."

She met his eyes rather defiantly, and saw that they had softened a little. With the change in their expression, his lean, tanned face was not quite so formidable.

"What happened?" he asked abruptly.

"I came out too far—and the wind changed. I tried to turn and, somehow, the wind caught the sail, and the yard-arm snapped just like a match-stick. I didn't know what to do. . . ."

She broke off, looking at him doubtfully.

"Well, I suppose you did the best thing under the circumstances—held on to the tiller and kept her clear of the islands," he observed without much enthusiasm for her seamanship. "Where are you from?"

"Glen Solan."

"I fancied that," he replied. "You've drifted a good distance. I saw you when I was making for the Loch and knew that you were in difficulties, but this mist came down and it took me some time to find you again."

8

The white launch was cutting its way through the waves, while away behind them the brown sail of Arline's boat tossed hither and thither on the grey water and was carried steadily onwards to its doom. With a quick shudder she turned back to the man in the launch.

He had risen from his seat in the stern and was bending over the engine again. The rhythmic beat of the small engine had changed its tempo, and something about it stirred a new fear in Arline's heart. Something had gone wrong.

The man turned and fumbled below the stern seat, producing two empty petrol tins which he flung on the floor boards with a look of disgust.

"Well," he said, "I told you not to thank me until I had delivered you safely on land again."

"You mean—there's no petrol?"

"Exactly."

His tone was curt again, and he frowned as he bent to the engine. Arline's heart began to hammer in her breast until she felt sure that it must drown the last feeble beat of the small motor. Her rescuer straightened and surveyed her across the width of the boat.

"I'm afraid you are in much the same predicament as you were half an hour ago," he said.

Arline flushed.

"This is all my fault," she began, "and now I've dragged you into it, too! I suppose it's useless to say I'm sorry."

He waved her apology aside.

"I'm afraid that won't help matters at the moment," he said rather abruptly. "I had no idea that I was without extra petrol. I didn't expect to come so far."

She knew that he must have been almost at his destination when he had noticed her, and had come out of his way to rescue her. It was not surprising, therefore, that he had run out of petrol.

"What can we do?" she asked rather lamely.

"Exactly what you were doing in the other boat," he said. "Keep her head-on to the wind, and hope for the best."

"And the best?" she questioned.

"That some other boat may see us and pick us up," he replied shortly. "Either that or else that we can land on one of the islands."

"Is that—possible?" she asked.

"Oh, yes—quite," he assured her. "We may even be lucky enough to find that the inhabitants have a boat which they may care to lend us,"

She knew that he must be angry, but it was hardly her fault that the launch was without petrol. Of course, it was her fault that he was forced to be here at all, she reflected quickly, and felt the hot colour staining her cheeks as she met his level gaze.

"Your people?" he questioned. "Are they likely to miss you?"

For the first time since she had come aboard the white launch Arline thought of her aunt. Mrs. Penner would undoubtedly miss her as soon as she rose from her afternoon nap, but her anxiety would be so tempered with annoyance that a hue and cry might be not be raised for many hours.

"No," she said at last, "I don't think they'll miss me for some time yet."

"Then they had no idea that you were out in the boat?" he asked.

"No—none whatever."

The thought of the lost boat sent a shiver of apprehension through her, and the man leaned forward and said more kindly:

"Don't worry, we're sure to be spotted before long by some boat coming up the Firth."

Those few words—the first really kind ones he had addressed to her—almost unnerved her. She felt a rush of tears to her eyes, and it was almost more than she could do to control them. She turned away a little, and looked out across the water.

They were drifting slowly towards a small island that rose out of the sea before them until they could see the full length of it through the thin mist. It looked rocky and dangerous as they approached, but Arline noticed that it sloped down to a level stretch of white sand at its southernmost point.

She glanced at her companion, and saw that his eyes were screwed up in contemplation of the narrow strip of land.

"You think we should go ashore?" she asked.

"I think we are going to have a very little choice," he replied.

Almost as he spoke a gust of wind caught them and drove them steadily onwards.

The man turned to her swiftly and gave her a searching glance.

"Can you hold on to the tiller while I keep her off these rocks with the boat-hook?" he asked.

Arline, feeling that he strongly doubted her ability to do so, took his place in the stern without a word. Her hands, already scarred by the ropes of the lug-sail, gripped hard on the tiller.

He seemed to be concentrating all his energy on saving the launch, and she thought quite suddenly that perhaps the loss of his boat would be as great a catastrophe for him as the wreck of her own small craft appeared to her. She wondered for the first time who he was.

His strong, bronzed face and firm, brown hands suggested a life spent mostly out of doors. His trousers were old and rather shabby, she noticed, but the grey polo sweater was good, but showed definite signs of wear at the elbows. He was hatless, and his dark hair was brushed back from his high forehead in a fruitless effort to subdue the waves in it. She came swiftly to the conclusion that he must be a yacht-hand up from Oban for the regatta which was being held in Loch Salon the following Saturday.

Her companion jumped down into the shallow water, and pulled the boat further up the beach until he was sure that it was in no danger of drifting away. Then, turning to her swiftly, he held out his arms.

"Come," he said, "there's no need for you to get your feet wet."

For an almost imperceptible second she hesitated, then she put her arms around his shoulders and permitted him to wade through the water with her to the dry sand. He set her on her feet and turned back to the boat, which he proceeded to pull as far up the beach as he could. When he returned Arline said quickly:

"I'm so glad you managed to save the launch. I should never have forgiven myself if anything had happened to it."

He turned to her.

"Yes, I'm glad I managed to land her without mishap," he said. "I hate endangering other people's property."

"I suppose your employer would have been very severe if anything had happened to it," Arline said.

He glanced at her with a puzzled expression in his grey eyes, and then the ghost of a smile twitched the corner of his mouth.

"Yes, I expect—the owner would have been most severe," he said.

"I know my uncle will be very angry when he finds out about his boat," she went on, with a catch at her throat as she thought of the scene which must surely follow her safe return to "Braeside."

"Surely your people will be only too glad to have you back safe and sound without troubling about the boat?" he remarked.

Arline shook her head with a little wry smile.

"I'm afraid not. I—you see, I had no right to be out in it unaccompanied," she explained.

"But that's ridiculous!" he flashed back. "Of course, you realise that you might quite easily have been drowned?"

She looked up at him.

"Yes, I do realise that, and—and I want to thank you for what you have done for me."

She held out her hand, but he did not seem to see it.

"I wonder what you will say when I tell you that I have probably landed you in a greater predicament," he said slowly.

He was scanning the mass of rocks before them and, as he did so, his dark brows drew together in a quick frown.

"What is it?" she asked.

He drew in his breath sharply.

"It looks as if we've struck one of the uninhabited islands of the group," he said, his voice gruff again, though his grey eyes were quite kindly when he looked down at her. "I'm sorry," he apologised.

"What can we do?" she asked.

He drew in a breath of relief at her tone.

"First of all," he said, "we can explore and see if things are really as bad as they seem."

She turned to walk across the sand by his side.

"What do you expect to find?" she inquired, trying to infuse a lightness into her tone which she was far from feeling.

He shrugged expressively, thrusting his hands deep into his trouser pockets.

"Nothing," he replied.

"But," Arline objected, "there might be a croft—or something—on the other side."

"If so, the people who built it were certainly mad!" he remarked. "Unless, of course, they possessed the kind of sheep that thrive on rocks and sea-weed!"

Arline was forced to laugh in spite of herself.

They clambered over the rocks in silence after that, and once or twice the man paused and turned to help her over a difficult stretch. The firm clasp of his hand renewed her confidence as they climbed higher and emerged eventually on a flat plateau where grass grew sparsely between the scattered boulders.

"I believe we could signal from here," he said hopefully. "If this mist would lift a bit there's just a chance that we might be seen."

"Look!" Arline pointed away to the south where the curtain of mist was slowly rolling back. "Isn't there—something out there?"

Her companion gazed into the distance for several seconds before he spoke.

"Yes, I believe there is! Come along, we'll go down and see."

She followed him quickly, leaping from rock to rock in his footsteps as they went down on the other side of the island. He halted on a narrow ledge of rock and looked out across the sea. The mist had dispersed before a rising wind, and they could plainly see the outline of another island lying before them. It appeared to be much larger than the one on which they had been stranded, and somewhere to the west the sun had broken through the clouds and was shining on what appeared to be the white gable of a house.

13

"Oh, look!" Arline cried. "Do you think that can be a croft?"

"It could be," he said, and for the first time she saw him smile.

The sense of relief which the distant view of human habitation brought sent an answering smile to her lips.

"How are we going to get across?" she asked eagerly.

"We'll signal. If this mist holds off for a while they're bound to see us and send help." He glanced down at the bright yellow triangle of silk which she wore about her neck. "May I borrow your scarf?" he asked.

She slipped it over her head.

"Certainly. Shall I take off my coat and wave that, too?"

"No, I believe the scarf will be enough," he smiled.

To Arline's immense relief the mist lifted completely, leaving a clear view of the island before them, with its stretch of sand so like their own and the little white croft nestling on the lee side of a tiny cove. The gable end of the house was towards them, and it was difficult to see from that distance whether there was any sign of habitation or not. There was certainly no sign of life, animal or human, on any other part of the second island.

"Do you think we should climb higher up and wave from there?" Arline asked at last.

"No, I believe they will see us from here—if they are going to see us at all."

When he had waved for almost half an hour without result, he handed the silk triangle back to her and prepared to descend to the shore again.

"You—think it isn't much use?" she questioned, following close behind him.

"I think we must do something more constructive," he replied.

"What do you propose to do?"

They had reached the level sand now, and he turned to her abruptly.

"Swim across and see just what *is* over there." He nodded in the direction of the croft."

"You can't," she said huskily. "The sea—it's so rough, and there may be all manner of currents sweeping through between the islands."

"I'll have to chance that," he replied. "Besides, I'm a fairly powerful swimmer and it's no great distance."

She looked at the grey sea, and the waves which dashed between the islands seemed mountainous to her troubled eyes.

"Please don't attempt it," she implored. "I can't expect you to risk your life for me."

"There won't be a great risk," he assured her with a faint smile, "and, after all, it's better than standing here doing nothing."

He took her arm and led her back across the shingle to the higher ground.

"I'll take you back to the launch and make you comfortable and perhaps by that time the tide will have gone out a bit and I won't have so far to swim."

She could not be sure whether his light tone was assumed or not, but she let it assure her, and followed him back across the rocks to where the white launch lay up on the beach. He picked up a yellow oilskin from the locker under the stern seat and held it out to her.

"Perhaps you'd better put this on," he suggested. "It's getting rather cold, and you may have some time to wait before I can get back with help."

Arline struggled into the big coat which came down almost to the toes of her white shoes.

"Thank you," she said a little more steadily, and tried to smile so that he would not think her afraid.

"Perhaps you had better sit in the launch," he suggested. "It will be more comfortable there."

"I will—afterwards, if you don't mind," she replied. "I think I'd rather walk about a little first. I—won't go very far."

She felt a desperate need for action, even if it were only the action of walking a little way along the shore, and waving the yellow scarf in the faint hope that it might be seen by some passing boat.

He called down to her from the rocks above, assuring her that it would not be long before he returned with help, and she answered him somehow, cheerfully.

When he was completely out of sight she walked northwards to the end of the curve of sand, and stood on a flat rock waving her yellow scarf until her arms ached. She began to wonder what time it was, and, realising that there was a small clock in the launch, went back to see. But, the little eight-day chronometer had stopped either the day before or many weeks past.

Sitting down on the brown leather cushions beneath the green awning, she looked about her. Even her inexperienced eye could detect that it was a well-built and beautifully turned out little craft. No wonder her rescuer felt anxious for its safety! Swiftly she reviewed the events of the past two hours. The moment when she had first hoisted the sail on her uncle's boat seemed very far away now. So many things had happened in that short space of time, and even now she was not quite at the end of her adventure.

Suddenly, high above her, a sea-gull screamed, wheeling out over the grey water, and the cry was like a warning.

She moved quickly, struggling to her feet, her eyes seeking the high rocks over which her companion had disappeared more than half an hour ago. When she saw him coming back towards her she could not believe the evidence of her own eyes for a moment, but he held up his hand reassuringly and she found herself waving in return.

He was rather breathless when he reached her, as if he had been running or scrambling across the rocks.

"What has happened?" she asked quickly.

"Something quite unexpected," he told her with a smile. "I should really have thought of it before now." He sat down on the gunwhale of the launch and made room for her beside him, but Arline remained on her feet, expectant, waiting.

"Yes—yes?" she urged.

"When I got over to the other side of the island I discovered that the tide had gone out a good deal further than I had expected," he went on, "and suddenly it occurred to me that, if I waited long enough, I might find that the small channel between the islands was an easily negotiable ford."

Arline drew in her breath in a quick sigh of relief.

"Oh," she said, "I'm so glad you've come back."

"I thought I may as well come and tell you," he remarked lightly.

"Then, if we can walk across at low tide, I can come with you?" she asked, her relief evident in eyes and voice.

"Yes, we can go across together."

She knew that he was making light of the situation for her sake, and thanked him inwardly for his consideration. All his former impatience had gone, and though his face in repose was still grave, the stern line had gone from his mouth and his eyes were quite friendly when they looked down into hers.

"I think you should keep that coat on," he advised, as they prepared to walk back to the other side of the island. "It might help to protect you a little."

"What about you?" Arline asked.

He laughed lightly.

"I never feel the cold. The weather has very little effect on me."

"I suppose you are out in all sorts of weather," she remarked, as they climbed upwards from the beach.

"Yes—frequently," he admitted.

"It must be very exciting to be on a racing yacht," she went on eagerly. "Is your—employer competing in the regatta on Saturday?"

"Yes, the *Ganta* will be racing on Saturday," he assured her with a smile.

It seemed to Arline that the journey to the other side of the island passed more swiftly this time, and soon they were standing on the wet sand watching the tide as it lapped in shallow ripples across a narrow neck of land.

"It can't be much more than a foot deep in the middle now," he said. "Shall we chance it?"

She nodded eagerly, and they set out together across the shining sand, leaving four wet footprints as evidence of their passing. When they came to the water her rescuer looked down at Arline's thin shoes and, without question, picked her up bodily into his arms.

It was the second time that he had held her that day, and she could feel the magnificent strength of him as he carried her without effort and set her down on the dry sand on the other side.

The beach sloped steeply here, with jagged rocks cropping out at intervals among the sand, and there was an air of loneliness about the place that they could not fail to feel.

The small white croft was hidden from view by a clump of stunted trees at this level, and Arline followed her

17

rescuer towards them with her first faint twinge of mis-giving. The place was so still and silent, and the sea-gulls whirled close above their heads as if their reign on the island had long been undisputed. She felt herself hanging back a little when the man pressed forward up the incline, and she let him go on alone when they reached the screening belt of trees.

He had gone no further than the gable end of the cottage, however, when she caught up with him, and the look on his face was enough to confirm the truth which she already knew in her heart.

Her eyes went beyond him.

The croft was even smaller than she had expected from their brief glimpse of it from the other island. It was in a bad state of disrepair, the thatch of the roof torn away in places by successive gales. The one door lay open, and the tiny windows on either side of it were devoid of glass or shutter. The dejected air of the place made Arline shiver involuntarily and draw a little nearer to her companion. She glanced up at him, and he turned quickly and pushed the door open with his foot.

"Well, here it is," he said, and, bending his head, passed through the low doorway into the one room beyond.

He returned almost immediately, his face grave, his mouth set in a firm line.

"It looks as if there hasn't been anyone here for a very long time," Arline said, conscious that the fact was obvious, but feeling that she must break the silence some-how.

Her companion turned to her slowly, and his eyes were completely devoid of expression as he said:

"We can signal again from the top of the hill, but I'm afraid there's going to be nothing else for it but to spend the night here."

18

CHAPTER TWO

THE NIGHT IN THE CROFT

I

GAVIN SHANDON remembered long afterwards how pluckily the girl took the news. Apart from the slow draining of colour from her face, Arline gave very little sign of the dismay she felt. No single thought dominated her mind in those first moments, but a series of disconnected doubts and fears seemed to file through her brain like a procession of tiny imps all intent on presenting themselves at their blackest.

Then, out of all the maelstrom of her conflicting thoughts and emotions, one very simple fact emerged—she was hungry. The long hours in the open air had produced this very natural result.

"Do you know," she said, with a little laugh, "I'm hungry?"

A look of intense relief spread across Shandon's face, and he even joined in her laughter.

"What do the very best castaways do in the novels?" he asked.

"Well, of course, they always have the most outrageous luck," she began.

"I know," he interrupted, "they find a case of canned foods, and the sea throws up most of the wreckage of their boat!"

"And the island is simply overflowing with bread-fruit trees and edible vines, and there's always a spring of clear water . . ."

"I'm afraid our island isn't going to yield a decent shelter for you for the night even," he said gravely. "There isn't a thing in the croft but an old table and a terribly rusty frying-pan. However, we might find the spring of clear water if we look around. The people who built the croft must have had a source of fresh water somewhere."

They went in search of the spring, and found it without very much trouble gurgling out of a rocky basin about a hundred yards from the front door. Arline cupped her hands together and drank gratefully, while the man watched the dark ripples of her hair and her slim form reflected dimly in the white-sanded spring and thought that she was the most beautiful thing he had ever seen.

She stood up at last and shook the hair back from her forehead.

"Still hungry?" he asked.

She nodded, drying her hands on the handkerchief which he offered for the purpose. She knew that behind his mask of gaiety he was thinking rapidly, and was not surprised when he said:

"I've thought all round this position, and I think our best plan would be to get what we can over from the launch to make you as comfortable as possible for the night. At least the croft will provide a small measure of shelter."

"If the mist lifts we may still be able to signal," Arline said hopefully.

"Yes—if it lifts. Meanwhile, I must go back to the launch before the tide begins to turn. It's almost low water now."

He turned towards the screen of trees, but Arline caught his arm.

"Please let me come with you," she begged. "I—I can always help to carry the crates of food back!" she added, with a little nervous laugh.

He did not object, and led the way down to the beach, where the tide had receded so far that they could walk across a comparatively dry stretch of sand to the smaller island beyond.

The launch was a friendly landmark as they climbed over the rocks towards their original landing-place. Shandon began to divest it of the brown cushions and, to his evident satisfaction, found a tartan rug flung carelessly in the bow. It was Arline who, stooping to close the door of the locker, discovered what she declared laughingly to be their greatest asset.

"What is it?" Shandon asked.

"Almost a complete half-pound block of milk chocolate!" she informed him with fitting gravity.

"Which," he observed solemnly, "will keep the wolf from the door for you for a few hours more."

So, in this light spirit of banter, they retraced their steps once more, Shandon going first with the cushions from the launch, and Arline following with the tartan plaid and the precious chocolate.

They picked up quite a lot of drift-wood on the way, and when they reached the croft, Shandon lit a smouldering and exceedingly smoky fire in the broken grate.

"The smoke may help to attract attention to us if it isn't much use as a means of warmth," he explained, as he accepted his share of the chocolate from Arline, who had insisted on dividing it into two equal portions.

"This luxury!" she murmured, munching her share eagerly.

He put the cushions on the rough wooden bench which ran along one wall of the croft, spreading the tartan plaid over them.

"This should be quite comfortable," he said, when he straightened from his task. "I hope you will be able to sleep a little."

"I—I may do."

"I'm going back to the launch," he said decisively. "You will be quite safe here. I won't sleep, and I'll be able to keep an eye on things from my side."

She slipped out of the yellow oilskin and held it out to him.

"You must take this," she said. "You see, I have the rug and—I'll be all right."

It had been an effort, that last rush of seeming confidence, but she had made it as much for her own sake as for his.

He picked up her yellow scarf.

"May I take this? I may need to signal again in the morning," he explained.

Arline went with him to the very edge of the water and they waited there together while the tide came in slowly and covered the sand until it was almost knee-deep at the centre when he waded across at last. They stood for a long time shouting instructions to one another until it was almost too dark to see across the lane of water which divided them.

She knew that he would be there all night, watching her shelter, and ready to come to her assistance at her first call, but when she turned away towards the crofter's hut, her heart was beating madly and the fear of the unknown had gripped her.

The fire was still smouldering in the grate, and she stirred it with a long piece of driftwood. There was a clammy coldness about the interior of the hut and she shivered and drew the tartan plaid round her shoulders, but she could not bring herself to lie down on the improvised bed.

Her thoughts turned quite naturally to her rescuer. She thought of him in the several moods he had presented to her during their brief acquaintance: the stern, unbending demeanour of their first encounter which had been so near to anger; the half-grudging admiration of her pluck and ready obedience when he had transferred her safely to his own boat; the softer, more friendly gleam in his grey eyes as he had gradually forgotten his first irritation, and, finally, the gentle courtesy with which he had made provision for her for the night.

She wondered idly whom he worked for, and experienced a keen desire to know more about him. It was difficult to realise that their acquaintance was only of a few hours standing. Thrown together under such circumstances, hours seem to take on the significance of years. In a curiously intimate way she seemed to have known him all her life.

She began to wonder what time it was, and went to the door to look out. Time—the time of clocks and ordered everyday life—mattered very little in such a situation, she thought, as she gazed out over the stunted trees to the shadowy outline of the other island. Though she could not see the stretch of sand from where she stood, the reassuring thought of Shandon's presence there helped to steady her. Quite easily she could picture him sitting on a flat boulder, or pacing the level stretch of beach, very wideawake and alert, his steady grey eyes never wavering from the line of thatch which was all that he could see of the little croft.

She knew, subconsciously, that she was very safe in his keeping, and with a little sigh of utter weariness she turned back into the hut and lay down on the cushions which he had spread for her.

The sun was pouring in through the glassless windows of the croft when Arline opened her eyes the following morning. For a moment she could not recall her thoughts as she rubbed her eyes sleepily and blinked at the bright light. Then realisation came flooding back to her as she took in her surroundings and stretched her cramped limbs.

Flinging the tartan plaid aside, she crossed to the window and looked out.

A fresh breeze met her, laden with the tang of salt, and she could see the blue waters of the Firth sparkling under the early morning sun, as if the new day was determined to banish all memory of the night before with its mist and darkness.

Pulling open the door, she stepped out into the sunshine. It was very early, but the stillness of the island had a peacefulness which was soothing to her jarred nerves. She walked to the spring and splashed the ice-cold water into her face, drying it on Shandon's handkerchief which she had kept from the night before. She stretched her hands high above her head, and for a moment the sheer beauty of the place held her in its spell until she thought that she would never forget the glory of that May morning as long as she lived.

Then the dark cloud of her impending return to civilisation drifted across her horizon, and she turned away from the sea with its prancing, white-crowned waves to the screen of trees which separated her from the other island.

Shandon was standing on a ledge of rock high up on his own side of the narrow channel, her yellow scarf in his hand as if he had been signalling for some time. He saw her almost immediately, and waved her to come across.

The tide was nearly out again, and Arline slipped off her shoes and stockings and waded the short distance to the other shore. He helped her up on the ledge beside him.

"Well, how did you sleep?" he asked, with an air of cheerfulness which she knew was for her benefit.

"Surprisingly well," she admitted with an answering smile. "And you?"

He made a deprecating gesture with his hands.

"It was really too beautiful a night to go to sleep once the mist rolled off," he replied.

23

"No luck yet, I suppose?" she asked, indicating the yellow scarf.

"Not so far," he replied, "but it can't be very long before life begins to stir over there."

He indicated the blurred coastline of the mainland with a nod of his dark head.

"Isn't it queer how the morning makes everything look —not quite so bad?" Arline remarked, bending to dry her feet. "Last night I had the feeling that the end of the world had come. It appeared as if we were thousands of miles from anywhere."

"I expect that was the psychological effect of the mist cutting us off completely," he replied, as he stooped to tie her shoe for her. "I wonder how far enquiries have gone for your safety?"

Arline started involuntarily.

"I—I don't know."

"I hope your people aren't too alarmed. Of course, it's bound to give them a bit of a shock," he said.

"And your—employer?" Arline asked.

Shandon smiled.

"Thank heaven, I'm alone at the moment and there will be no extensive enquiries on my account!"

She felt relief for his sake. At least he would not suffer in any way for coming to her rescue.

He fastened her second shoe securely for her and stood up to look out to sea again, shading his eyes with his hand against the sun.

"Ah," he said at last, still gazing into the distance, "I might have thought of that."

"Of what?" Arline asked.

"The fishing fleet," he replied, turning back to her. "We didn't see them go out last night simply because they take the other side of the islands."

"You mean—they're coming in now?"

"Yes—right down the Firth. You'll see the first one in a minute. Look! Over there."

Arline shaded her eyes and picked out half a dozen small specks on the blue water away to the south.

"Oh, yes," she cried. "Do you think they'll see us?"

"We must make them see us," he said. "Come along. We'll climb a little higher and make absolutely sure."

He helped her over the rough ground, and they stood on a small grassy patch and waved the scarf and Shandon's handkerchief. Neither spoke. The same thought was in the mind of each: would they be seen, or would the fishing fleet pass on without noticing them?

They counted seven boats in all, plying their way swiftly up the Firth in the direction of Loch Solan. One by one they drew level with the islands, and one by one they passed without giving any sign. The men, busy with their work on deck, had not seen their frantic signalling.

Shandon let his arm fall to his side.

"Well, that's another hope gone. These fellows must be blind!"

"I suppose they're so busy they have little time to gaze around them, and they'll be able to steer their course almost automatically by now," Arline observed.

"Yes, I suppose so," he agreed. "Still, our luck might have held out and let one of them notice us!"

"It *has* held out!" Arline caught him by the arm in her excitement. "Look! Look!"

Two fishing boats had come into view round the end of the second island and were cutting out across the Firth to follow the fleet into the loch. They were much nearer than the fleet had been, and it was next to impossible for them not to notice the stranded launch.

Gavin Shandon took no chances, however, and while Arline waved both scarf and handkerchief, he began to shout lustily to attract their attention.

Almost immediately there was an answering signal from the first boat, and she left her course and came round towards the island.

Arline's heart was beating madly.

"Oh—they've seen us at last," she cried, all her relief echoing in her voice.

Shandon looked down at her with a curious mixture of pleasure and regret in his grey eyes.

"Yes," he said slowly, "our adventure is over."

The fishing boat was making rapid progress towards them, and he led the way down on to the beach where the white launch lay in the early morning sunshine like a giant bird poised on the edge of the waves.

There were three men in the fishing boat, all attired in the blue jersey and cloth cap of the fisherman, with their sleeves rolled up above their elbows, and their hands red from their night's toil. Arline could see the name of the boat in white letters along the bow—the *Mary Bella*. She remembered seeing the boat moored to the side of the quay at Loch Solan.

Shandon was shouting his request for help across the intervening water, and one of the men called back that they had no spare petrol, but that they could take them aboard the fishing-boat and tow the launch to the loch.

"Never mind the launch," Shandon shouted. "Can you get us aboard now?"

"I'll need to be takin' ye off the rocks yonder," one of the men decided.

Shandon turned to Arline.

"We'll have to walk back to the rocks and get on from there," he explained. "The men can't bring their boat into shallow water in case they ground her."

He led the way quickly across the beach to where the rocks jutted out into the sea. As if it had been made for their purpose, a wide shelf of rock went out into comparatively deep water, and the fishermen steered their boat alongside.

A plank was put down between the boat and the rocky shelf, and over this unsteady gangway Shandon helped his companion. Two hard, wet hands caught her outstretched ones, and she was guided to a seat in the *Mary Bella*.

The two younger fishermen went silently to work, but the owner of the boat plied Shandon with questions.

"Would ye be from Loch Solan, then?" he asked, eyeing them both with frank curiosity.

"Yes," Shandon replied. "Can you put us in there?"

"Indeed I can that," the man replied. "And how would you be gettin' stranded up on the island?"

Arline noticed that Shandon was smiling faintly at the other's curiosity.

"This lady had an accident with her boat and I went to her assistance," he explained briefly. "Afterwards I discovered that I had run out of petrol and the launch was driven on to the island."

26

His tone conveyed that he had told them all there was to know of the little adventure, and Arline was surprised at how quickly he managed to steer the conversation round to the night's catch and the history of the *Mary Bella*.

He came over and sat down beside her when they rounded the Point and went more slowly down the loch.

"Feeling hungry again?" he asked lightly.

"Not—so much," she replied, conscious that her thoughts were racing too swiftly ahead to her home-coming to permit of any desire for food.

"You will do when you get home and see everything set out on the table. We should just be in time for a good breakfast."

The fishing fleet was already moored and, in spite of the early hour, there was great activity along the little stone fish quay that ran parallel to the pier. More activity than usual, Arline thought, as she noticed the small groups of women gathered along the quay.

As the *Mary Bella* drew nearer the women edged up the landing-stage, and Arline realised swiftly that the story of their rescue had reached Glen Solan before them. The *Mary Bella's* companion boat had gone on ahead and had broken the news.

Shandon, too, seemed quick to grasp the situation, and Arline felt his hand clasp firmly under her elbow as the ropes were thrown to the quay and a dozen eager hands stretched out to moor this suddenly-important fishing boat.

The women were standing back now in silent groups, making a great pretence of not looking, but conscious of every movement just the same. Arline felt that she wanted to run—swiftly—anywhere away from these furtive, watching eyes.

When he jumped to the quay after her Shandon guided her firmly and deliberately away from the crowds.

"Perhaps it would be better if I came home with you," he suggested, and the level tone of the quiet voice helped her to control her own as she replied:

"No—thank you all the same. I think it would be better if I went alone. I—it will be easier to explain," she added hurriedly.

"Just as you wish," he replied.

"You won't think me ungrateful," she went on. "It was very kind of you to offer and, in other circumstances, I would have been only too willing to accept, but—but, you see, my aunt is inclined to be—a little strict. I think it would be much better if I went on alone, if you don't mind."

Her distress was evident to the man by her side, and his dark brows drew together in a quick frown.

"Perhaps I'd better come if they're going to make a fuss," he said sharply.

"No—no, it will be all right—really it will," she said, trying to infuse a note of assurance into her voice. "After all, I haven't done anything criminal."

There was determination in her tone, and her chin lifted a little as if she had made up her mind to stand her ground at the forthcoming interview. Gavin Shandon, who had already formed a mental picture of her relatives, thought that his companion of the island might not come off second-best after all.

As they approached the end of the quay where the fish boxes stood piled up against the whitewashed wall a boy came running towards them and pulled up in front of them.

"Oh—Dougie!" Arline cried, then, turning to her companion, she explained quickly: "This is my cousin."

Douglas Penner held out a long, brown hand and clasped Shandon's.

"The name is Shandon—Gavin Shandon. It's quite time I introduced myself!" Shandon said with a smile.

"How d'you do!" Douglas replied, while he continued to gaze at the other with frank curiosity. Then, deciding very suddenly that he liked his cousin's rescuer, he went on: "It was deuced fortunate that you were there to pick her up, I should say. I guess you really saved her life."

"I wouldn't put it as strongly as that," Shandon replied, with a warm smile which returned a verdict in Douglas' favour. "Anyway, I'm going to turn her over to you now, so see that you take good care of her."

His tone was light, and Arline felt that he did not want her to thank him again. However, she attempted to do so, and holding out her hand, said warmly:

"I can't begin to thank you for all you have done— but I am really grateful."

28

He took her hand in a friendly clasp.

"Shall we consider the debt settled, then?" he said kindly. Douglas tucked his hand into her arm.

"Come on, Arline—before the crowd starts to gather again," he urged. "I've answered more questions this morning than I've done in the course of my short lifetime!"

Shandon stepped aside to let them pass, and stood looking after them as they went side by side up the hill.

There was a faint smile playing about the corners of his firm mouth, and his grey eyes held the same half-whimsical expression that had been in them when Arline had expressed her hope that his employer would not be too severe over the adventure with the launch.

II

"And now," said Douglas, panting slightly with the exertion of his climb from the quay, "what exactly happened—and how?"

Arline, roused from her preoccupation by the question, slowed down a little.

"Well," she said rather breathlessly, "you know I took the boat out after lunch."

"Yes, I know that part. Mother had been pitching into you again, I suppose?"

Arline was silent. She knew that she had her young cousin's sympathies, but she rarely complained to him of his mother's conduct.

"Go on," he encouraged.

"Well, I got the sail up and everything went fine while I was in the bay. Then I struck a small-sized gale just beyond the Point. I tried to remember all you had ever told me, Dougie, and I believe I was getting her round fine when an outsize in waves hit me broadside on."

"Good heavens!" Douglas ejaculated, "did it swamp you?"

"No, not quite. I managed to hold on, but the yard snapped and I was helpless."

Recounting it thus to a sympathetic listener brought each detail of the adventure back vividly to her.

"Yes?" Douglas prompted, coming to a halt on the steep hill path, so that they would not reach "Braeside" before he had heard the end of the tale.

"Well, I was desperately afraid, of course, and I had no idea what was going to happen to me, and then that dreadful mist came down and cut me off completely."

"Where did the rescue come in?" he asked eagerly.

"Just as I was sure I was going to drift on to one of the islands and be smashed up on the rocks," she told him.

"He had a boat, of course?"

"Yes—a motor-launch. Oh, Dougie, I was never more pleased to see anyone in all my life."

"But, that was yesterday, Fair Cousin!" he remarked lightly.

"Yes—yes, I know. I'm coming to—to the other bit."

"Well, go ahead. I promise not to interrupt again."

"On our way back," Arline began hesitatingly, "he found that he had run out of fuel. There wasn't enough in the launch to do the return journey."

"Hadn't he an auxiliary pair of oars?"

"Evidently not—and no spare petrol. You see, he was returning to Loch Solan and had just enough to take him there when he saw me," Arline explained. "I don't suppose he stopped to think about his fuel supply when he saw me drifting. Besides, I believe he thought there was a spare tin somewhere in the launch."

"Terribly awkward," Douglas acknowledged. "What did he do?"

"He was forced to land on one of the islands, or else we might have drifted very much further south," Arline went on. "You see, we thought we might strike an inhabited one."

"And was it?"

She shook her head.

"No——"

"I say! What an adventure! Cast away on a deserted island with a tall and handsome stranger."

"Don't, please, Dougie!" she said.

"Sorry," Douglas apologised immediately. "But—who is he?"

"A yacht-hand from one of the yachts in the bay, I think."

Douglas whistled.

"Are you sure?"

"I think so," Arline replied. "Why?"

"Oh, nothing!" airily. "I just fancied that he spoke rather well for a yacht-hand, that's all. Of course, you never know these days!"

Douglas turned as if to lead the way towards the house.

"Dougie," Arline called after him, "how did you find out? About the rescue, I mean?" she asked.

He turned back towards her with a reminiscent grin.

"I was terribly late for dinner to start with," he explained, "and, of course, it was thought that you were with me until I appeared solo about eight-thirty. Do you know, mother actually forgot to pitch into me for being late when she discovered you hadn't been with me at all."

"Then, you had no idea about the boat?" Arline asked.

"No," Douglas admitted, "it didn't seem to strike anyone until about midnight that you *might* have taken the boat. Honestly, Arline, when I went down to the boat-house and found it gone it was nearly the finish of me."

His genuine concern for her safety was very evident, and Arline gave his arm a little affectionate squeeze.

"After that," he continued, "there was a terrible rumpus. MacDonald and Father and I went out in Mac's boat and searched all along the shores of the loch as far as the Head and back again along to the Point. It wasn't very long before the dawn broke and we came back to get help in the village. Old Frazer promised to lend us his launch, and we came back up here for brandy and a few things to organize a proper search. Then, just as we were setting out again, Frazer's son came running to say you had been found on the island with——" Douglas hesitated.

"Yes, Dougie?" Arline prompted.

"Well—just with—a man."

There was a tense silence, broken at last as Arline turned towards the house and said quietly.

"Let's go in now, Dougie."

Douglas pushed the gate open for her and followed her up the short, steep drive.

"Braeside" stood before them, wrapped in what Arline imagined to be an ominous calm. The grey stone walls looked down at her coldly above the neat, terraced lawn, and the blinds were still down at most of the upstairs windows, which gave them the appearance of vacant eyes staring out across the loch.

Arline shivered involuntarily and, avoiding the use of the front door, walked round the gable end of the house towards the back entrance. Douglas followed her, whistling lustily to herald their approach. Arline wished for a moment that he would not make such a noise, for she would have liked to go to her own room for a few minutes before she encountered the rest of the family. However, she reflected that it did not matter very much, and was not surprised when finally she saw her uncle's portly form emerging from the old coach-house which had been converted into a garage.

Henry Penner had made his money out of sauce, a condiment that was never permitted to appear on the Penner dining-table lest it should remind the elder members of the family too forcibly of the days, long past, when they had made the first bottles of Penner's Famous Sauce in the back kitchen of a grocer's shop in Glasgow.

Henry regarded his niece out of his small, beady eyes for a moment without a word, then, drawing himself up with an effort, he said loudly:

"Arline—h'm—your aunt is waiting for you in her room. Please go up to her immediately. H'm."

He turned back towards the garage, and Arline gave Douglas a fleeting smile.

"I'll go in now," she said. "I'll see you—later."

On her way up to her aunt's small sitting-room on the first landing, she wondered for perhaps the hundredth time since she had come to live with the Penners how anyone like Uncle Henry could possibly have been her mother's brother. What strange tie of blood could possibly have linked two beings so utterly unlike each other? There was not even one single mannerism or one little feature of Henry Penner's which suggested relationship with the tall, patrician, gentle woman whom Arline remembered as her mother. Janice Hamilton had been a woman to whom all had come in time of trouble, though her own failing health might have been considered trouble enough by a less generous heart.

As she knocked at her aunt's closed door, Arline sighed and thought how different her home-coming would have been had she been able to run straight to the shelter of a mother's love.

"Come in."

The voice from within the room was barely audible, and Arline knew that she had stumbled upon one of her aunt's most difficult moods. She pushed open the door, closing it gently behind her.

Mrs. Penner was reclining on a low *chaise-longue* beside the window, the blind of which had been let down to its fullest extent to exclude the early morning sunlight, so that the room was bathed in a kind of suppressed golden glow which, in itself, appeared ominous to Arline. Her aunt wore a loose *négligé* with a bold flower design on it, and a handkerchief wrung out of eau-de-Cologne was laid over her eyes. She removed this carefully when Arline entered, and turned her piercingly blue eyes upon her niece.

For the space of a few seconds there was a dreadful silence in which neither spoke. Arline knew that her aunt's attitude would depend upon the pose she decided to adopt for the moment. When Mrs. Penner drew her long white hand across her forehead and emitted a heavy sigh, she was quite prepared for her aunt's first remark.

"To think that I should have lived to see this day!" Mrs. Penner breathed into the pile of cushions on which her immaculately-waved head rested.

"Aunt Hilda—I'm very sorry . . ." Arline began, but Mrs. Penner waved her apology aside.

"Sorrow—or anything else—can never undo the events of last night," she declared, her blue eyes full of accusation. "To think that I have brought up two children of my own —perfectly—and then that this should have to happen!"

She pressed the scrap of linen to her eyes again and gave another sigh. Arline, whose nerves were already strained almost to breaking point by the events of the past twenty-four hours, felt that she could not stand the farce of her aunt's attitude any longer.

"Aunt Hilda, I'm sorry, but I don't see that there is any need for all this fuss. Nothing has 'happened,' as you elect to put it, except that I have been rescued from a rather unpleasant death, and have returned here safe and

33

well at the very first opportunity to assure you of my safety."

There was an unconscious note of reproof in her voice, and Mrs. Penner sensed it immediately. Her attitude of hurt surprise at the "episode" dropped from her like a cloak, and she rose to her feet with an alacrity which belied her former lethargy. Her martyred expression changed to a hard and vindictive look as she crossed to her niece's side.

"Oh," she said sharply, "*you* don't think there's any need for fuss! I suppose you don't consider that staying on an island over-night with a man is in any way out of the ordinary?"

Arline flushed, but she was determined to remain calm.

"There was hardly time to pick up a chaperone, Aunt Hilda, when we were struggling for our lives," she said slowly.

Mrs. Penner drew back, a dull red colour mounting to her sallow cheeks.

"Of course," she reflected, "I might have expected such an attitude from you, Arline. You have, undoubtedly, inherited your father's utter disregard for the conventions."

"I don't think we need discuss my father at the moment," Arline said quietly. "After all, what happened was purely an accident. I am quite willing to be reprimanded for taking Uncle Henry's boat out without his permission, but, apart from that, I don't think I am in any way to blame for the—the accident."

"Indeed!" Mrs. Penner's tone was like the lash of a whip. "I'm glad you realise that you did wrong in the first place in taking the boat without permission, but I hope that I will be able to make you see that the remainder of your—adventure is equally blameworthy."

"I'm afraid I can't see that," Arline replied simply.

Mrs. Penner wheeled round and walked to the window, where she let the blind up with a jerk which sent it flapping to the top of the frame.

"I suppose that, too, is only to be expected. I could hardly hope that you might see *my* side of the question!" She paused, and once more the martyred look took pride of possession upon her face. "I'm sure I really don't know why I should be called upon to suffer this sort of thing at my age and in my state of health!"

Arline, who had never known her aunt to have been seriously ill during the whole of her lifetime, wondered what the remark was leading up to.

Mrs. Penner sighed again.

"Well, I suppose we must just get ready to leave as quietly as possible!" she said heavily.

"To leave Glen Solan?" Arline questioned. "But, Aunt Hilda—why?"

"Why!" Mrs. Penner's blue eyes were wide with incredulity at the question. "Surely you do not require to ask *why*, my dear Arline? You are no longer a child that I need to explain each little point to you!"

"I still don't see any need to leave," Arline said firmly, determined that her aunt should explain her attitude.

Mrs. Penner drew herself up to her full height.

"Then, perhaps the fact that I do may be sufficient reason," she said acidly. "I am beginning to make friends here, people whose friendship may be—whose friendship I value."

Ah, Arline thought, now we are coming round to the real reason, but she kept silent and let her aunt continue.

"Fortunately," Mrs. Penner went on, "the McCallum-Blairs are away from the Glen for a day or two and they may not hear of this—this disgraceful affair, but before they come back I must see that the villagers' memories of it are not refreshed by constant sight of you."

So this was the trouble. Arline could barely suppress a smile. Her aunt, aiming at social advancement, had been doing her best to make friends with the people who owned Dunsolan House, the great, rambling structure which crowned Solan Point. One meeting with Mrs. McCallum-Blair at the local Ladies' Club had only increased Mrs. Penner's desire for further friendship, and Arline knew that her aunt would do anything to achieve that end.

"Your uncle has agreed to close the house as soon as the regatta is over on Saturday," Mrs. Penner continued. "We will travel back to town on Monday morning." Having delivered her ultimatum, she turned to the door which led into her bedroom, pausing there to deliver her Parthian shot. "Perhaps it may interest you to know," she said icily, "that, by your action, you have spoiled Helen's chance to become acquainted with a very desirable family."

Though the Penners had made a success of their lives, as far as the acquisition of wealth can be considered success, they had never achieved any great social standing, and this fact was the one perpetual thorn in Mrs. Penner's flesh. She had long been determined that her only daughter, Helen, should marry well, and Arline sighed a little for quiet, wistful Helen as she made her way up to her own small bedroom at the back of the house. Helen would be offered up on the altar of her mother's ambition.

Arline could not visualise her aunt giving up the chance of further acquaintance with the McCallum-Blair's merely because of the incident on the island, but Mrs. Penner had certainly seemed determined to transfer the entire household from "Braeside," for the time being at any rate.

With a little, weary sigh, she pushed open the door of her own room and sank down on the small single bedstead.

Her aunt had made her feel that the whole family were being punished on her account. She knew that Douglas had been thoroughly enjoying his holiday in the Glen, and that Helen had colour in her pale cheeks which never appeared there in Glasgow.

Presently there came a light tap on the door and a girl's voice calling her by name.

"Arline—Arline, are you there?"

Arline swung her feet off the bed and sat up.

"Yes, Helen. Come in."

Helen Penner's fair head appeared round the door. There was a shy smile in her blue eyes as she met her cousin's dark ones, as if she were dumbly apologising for what she had heard of her mother's tirade. She slipped round the door and closed it gently behind her, coming softly across the room to sit down beside Arline on the bed.

"Oh, I'm so glad you're safe!" she whispered, as if she were half-afraid of being overheard. "What happened—exactly?"

"I took the boat out and was caught by the tide and the wind," Arline explained briefly. "Then—a man came to my rescue and on our way back to the loch we ran out of petrol and drifted on to the island."

"Oh, Arline—how romantic!" Helen laughed softly. "What was he like? Do say he was young and handsome."

Arline flushed, but she met her cousin's blue eyes steadily enough.

"He was young," Arline admitted.

"And handsome?" went on her fair inquisitor.

"Yes—I suppose you would call him handsome."

Helen sat back on the bed and hugged her knees.

"Does he live in Glen Solan?" she asked.

"I don't know. No—I suppose not."

"Oh, then he's just here on holiday?" Helen surmised.

"No, I think he must be here with one of the yachts for the regatta," Arline decided. "He told me he was going to race on Saturday.

"Oh, how interesting! Which is his yacht?" her cousin asked eagerly.

"I don't think he owns a yacht, Helen. You see, I think he's working here. He's one of the deck-hands, I fancy."

Helen was silent for a moment. Then:

"Are you going to see him again?" she asked.

Arline shook her head.

"I don't suppose so."

"I'm disappointed," Helen declared. "I thought I scented a romance!"

Before Arline could reply, Mrs. Penner's voice floated up to them from the landing below, demanding her daughter's presence immediately.

Helen was very pale as she scrambled from Arline's bed and said hurriedly:

"It's mother. I mustn't let her find me here!" She put one thin arm round her cousin's shoulder. "I'm so glad you are safely home, Arline."

The tears were bright in Arline's eyes as the door of her bedroom closed and she heard her cousin tip-toeing softly downstairs.

III

It was after nine o'clock before Arline, washed and changed and feeling very much refreshed, put in an appearance in the small morning-room. She had met a maid carrying a laden tray upstairs, and the girl had explained timidly that it was Mrs. Penner's breakfast.

Henry Penner was buried behind an old copy of *The Yachtsman*, but Arline had the feeling that he was not reading it; she could almost feel his small, beady eyes upon her round the edge of the periodical. She wondered what he would have to say about the loss of his boat, or if he had decided to leave all the reprimanding to his wife, suggesting and encouraging only when they were alone together.

Helen, having escaped her mother's eagle eye, had eaten a light breakfast and was standing by the long, open window looking out to the green freshness of the hills. Douglas, still seated at the table, made room for Arline beside him.

"I expect you're starving," he remarked cheerfully. "I've left you more than an average share of bacon, and you can have Helen's as well, by the look of things!"

Arline went over to the sideboard and helped herself, while Helen turned from the window to pour her coffee for her.

"Mother isn't feeling too well this morning," she explained Mrs. Penner's absence.

Arline, remembering the well-stocked tray which she had seen the maid carrying to her aunt's room, made no immediate reply.

There was an awkward, tense feeling about the atmosphere in the morning-room: none of them were wholly at ease. Arline wished, suddenly, that her uncle would speak, reprimand her—anything—or go out. He did not seem inclined to do either, however, and she finished her meal in silence.

Helen strolled out into the garden, and, as Arline pushed back her chair to follow her, Henry Penner lowered his paper and spoke for the first time. His tone was heavy and lumberingly sarcastic.

"Perhaps, when you have a moment to spare, you may give me some idea of what happened to my boat."

Arline flushed.

"Yes—yes, of course, I meant to, Uncle Henry," she began. "I—we were forced to let it go. The sea was so rough and there was danger of us swamping the launch."

"I see," Penner murmured. "I take it that you let her drift on to the rocks?"

"I don't know."

"Um-ph! I gather that this man you were with was able to save his own boat?"

A sudden anger kindled within Arline. Instead of being anxious to seek out Gavin Shandon to thank him for what he had done in saving her life, or trying to reward him in some way, all her uncle's concern was for his boat. She wondered if they realised how near death she had been when Shandon had come to her rescue.

"I said he seemed to find no difficulty in saving his own boat," Henry Penner repeated testily.

"Saving the launch was the first step towards saving my life," Arline replied with some spirit.

Henry Penner's little eyes fell before the direct gaze of his niece's dark ones.

"Yes—yes, of course, we realise that," he said quickly, "but the fact remains that boat cost me quite a lot of money, and I want to know what became of it."

On the last word his hand came down on the table with a bang which set the cutlery jangling. In spite of his wealth, Henry Penner was still mean over the little things, and his possessions were sacred to him. Arline, who had turned half-way to the window, came back towards the table.

"I will do my best to find out," she said quietly, anxious to avoid another scene. "Perhaps I shall be able to get some information down at the quay."

"There's no need for that."

Douglas, who had been a tight-lipped witness of the whole proceedings, rose to his feet and crossed to her side, slipping a friendly arm through hers.

"I don't think you should interfere in this," his father growled.

"There's no need for Arline to go down to the quay to enquire about a boat," Douglas replied steadily. "I'll see to that side of the business." He turned back to his cousin. "Leave it to me, Arline. And—don't worry!" he added, under his breath.

Henry Penner rose to his feet, scowling at his son, and strode through the open french window into the garden, the scarlet flush of suppressed anger showing even at the back of his short, flabby neck.

Douglas emitted a sigh which ended in a low whistle.
"Well, what now?"

Arline put her hand gently on his arm.

"Dougie, it was fine of you to—defend me, but don't get yourself into trouble on my account. After all, it *was* wrong of me to take the boat . . ."

"Wrong, fiddlesticks," Douglas broke in with a fine air of scorn. "It was no more wrong than if I had taken it myself. Why shouldn't you take the boat? You're one of the family, aren't you?"

Arline's lips curved in a little smile, but she shook her head.

"No, Dougie, and I'm afraid all I can do is to apologise."

"Apologies are discounted here," he declared. "I thought you would have found that out before now."

Arline did not reply, and they walked out into the garden in silence. She was conscious of Douglas holding her arm in a firm grasp, however, which assured her of his friendship more than any words could have done.

"It's very hard to know what to do," she said at last, coming out of her reverie. "There doesn't seem to be very much that I *can* do."

"There isn't," Douglas agreed, "except, perhaps, to seek out Shandon and—sort of reward him in some way."

Arline stopped suddenly.

"Dougie—we simply couldn't offer him money—if you're suggesting that."

"Why not?"

"I can't explain. He's just—not that type. He would take it as an insult—I'm sure of that."

"Yes, I guess you're right," Douglas admitted. "If I'm any judge of character, he'd slay any man on sight who suggested it."

"It seems such a small return just to say 'Thank you'," Arline mused, half to herself.

"Perhaps it's all the return he wants," Douglas suggested wisely. "Did you thank him properly?"

"I tried to."

He gave her a sidelong glance.

"I didn't hear you making an awfully good speech."

"You can't make pretty speeches when you are — excited," Arline defended herself.

"Well, you're not excited now," her cousin pointed out.

"Dougie, are you suggesting that I—should seek him out to—to thank him again?"

"Why not? After all, he saved your life, didn't he?"

There was a distinct twinkle in his blue eyes as they met hers, and for the first time in her life Arline was too confused to answer him. She shook her head at him instead, and as he went down the drive at an easy trot, he called back to her:

"Think it over. It's worth a thought, at least."

IV

Mrs. Penner did not appear for lunch, and Helen was summoned peremptorily to take that meal in her mother's room.

Arline had spent the morning on the green slope of lawn before the house since nobody seemed to have need of her services, and there had been very little post to attend to at eleven o'clock. From where she had been sitting on the long garden chair she could see the full expanse of the bay spread out before her in the bright sunshine.

Once, a white launch had sped out from the landing-stage, leaving a widening streak of wake behind it, and her thoughts had swung round again to Gavin Shandon. She wondered what he must think of her—if he was angry, or just indifferent. Perhaps he had even forgotten about her in the claim of other duties.

Her eyes roved back to the Point and the long sweep of grassy land which faced the bay. The McCallum-Blairs' big, white house, nestling in the sheltering arms of its surrounding trees, dominated the view from where she sat. It was a house with a benign and friendly countenance, Arline thought lazily, and her mental inspection passed on to its occupants. She wondered idly what the McCallum-Blairs were like.

Knowing how eager her aunt was to appear on friendly terms with them, Arline imagined that the two women must have something in common. Mrs. McCallum-Blair would quite probably be a more refined replica of her aunt Hilda.

41

She thought of Helen, and how anxious her mother was that she should marry well. That was more than likely the reason why Mrs. Penner wanted to cultivate the McCallum-Blairs' son. Poor Helen! Somehow Arline felt that her cousin had very little interest in her mother's matrimonial ambitions for her. There had been a look of frailty about Helen lately that only Arline seemed to have noticed; the winter behind them, with its attendant social functions, had appeared to tax Helen's strength to the utmost, and she had been unfeignedly glad to get away from the city.

Lunch was an unsatisfactory meal at any time at "Braeside," but although his mother was not present to remonstrate with him when he appeared quarter of an hour after the gong had sounded, Douglas seemed to feel the continued tension in the atmosphere as soon as he entered the dining-room. He sought to dispel it with his news.

"I say, we've had a bit of luck after all." His cheerful grin was for Arline, his information primarily for his father.

"And what is that?" Henry Penner asked, looking up from his plate.

"They've found the boat—and it's not too badly damaged."

"Oh—I'm so glad," Arline cried thankfully.

"Where did you hear this?" Mr. Penner asked.

"I've been down at the quay all morning, and about eleven o'clock Shandon — that's the fellow who rescued Arline—came in with his launch. Seemingly he had gone down the Firth in search of our boat, and found it high and dry on one of the other islands."

"Did he bring it off?" Henry asked abruptly.

"No. From what I could gather, it will need a bit of attention before it can be towed back," Douglas explained, "but Shandon says it can easily be repaired."

"Does this—Shandon know anything about boats?" Mr. Penner questioned.

"I should say he does. In fact, I would say he knew *everything* about them."

It was evident that Douglas had taken an immediate liking to Gavin Shandon.

"Well, I expect we can get him to bring it in for us. Find out what it will cost, Douglas, and let me know."

Mr. Penner pushed back his chair and went out through the small conservatory to the garden.

"The old man thinks money can buy anything!" Douglas observed lightly.

"Did—Mr. Shandon offer to bring the boat in?" Arline asked.

"As a matter of fact, he did," Douglas replied, passing his plate for a second helping. "He said it would be no trouble at all."

"But," Arline pointed out, "his employer might object."

"Well, he didn't seem to worry about that, so I just said it was very nice of him to offer and that we would be kind of pleased to get the boat back."

Arline moved uneasily in her chair.

"I don't like the way we all seem to be taking him for granted," she said quickly.

"He wants to help, I can assure you," Douglas replied, "and there's no sense in refusing an offer of assistance once it's made."

"No—perhaps not."

"I'm going to meet him again at two o'clock and we're taking a repair outfit with us. With any luck at all we should get her off at high tide."

"You'll be careful, Dougie?" Arline begged.

He gave her a friendly pat on the cheek.

"Imagine *you* talking about being careful in a boat," he laughed, as he ran upstairs to change.

That afternoon seemed the longest that Arline could remember. Helen came downstairs after lunch and said that she was going into Oban on an errand for her mother and was taking the car, though she did not invite Arline to accompany her.

"I'll be back before dinner," she said hurriedly, and went out in the direction of the garage.

When the car had purred away down the drive, Arline took a book out to the lawn. Her uncle had disappeared without dictating his usual batch of letters, and the garden was wrapped in the hush of the warm afternoon. There was little activity in the bay, and the only sound about her was the friendly chirping of the birds which swarmed among the trees and hopped across the lawn less than a yard from her chair.

43

Away out almost at the Point she could just distinguish a small white launch, and convinced herself that it must be Shandon's. Turning to her book, she read fitfully for an hour until she went indoors to supervise the tea.

Going up to her aunt's room, she tapped on the door.

"Who's there?" came the voice from within.

"Arline. May I come in?"

"What do you want?"

"I wondered if I could do anything for you, and—it's almost tea time."

They were still speaking with the door closed between them.

"There's nothing you can do"—petulantly. "I'm too distressed to come down for tea, and much too upset to see anyone. I don't think I'll even be able to come down for dinner."

Arline, who knew these moods so well, and had long ago decided that it was best to let them take their course, made no reply.

"Arline"—sharply from the inside of the door.

"Yes, Aunt Hilda?"

"Oh, I thought you had gone. You may tell Alice to bring my tea up to my room. That's all."

When she had waited for twenty minutes and neither Mr. Penner nor Douglas had put in an appearance, Arline carried her cup out to the lawn and sat sipping her tea in the shade of the trees. A terrible feeling of loneliness began to assail her, and she thought of Douglas and his companion and wondered what they were doing.

In a vague sort of way, and without seeking for a reason for the feeling, she was glad that Douglas had expressed his liking for her rescuer in no indefinite terms. It seemed to take some of the sting out of her aunt's attitude towards the incident of the island. She began to wonder about the boat, and at last, unable to sit still any longer, she went indoors and picked up her headscarf from the hall-stand. She did not put it on, but carried it in her hand, swinging it idly as she went down the drive and out on to the hill road.

Although she had set out with no very definite objective in mind, she was not surprised when her footsteps turned almost naturally towards the pier.

The village was practically deserted, for it was the tea hour, and the few men left on the various boats were all busy with their nets. Arline recognised the familiar lines of the white launch immediately. It was moored at the end of the small jetty, but it was unoccupied. She wondered if Shandon and Douglas had not gone out for the boat after all, and if she had been mistaken when she had thought that she had seen the launch from the house.

"Have you missed your cousin?"

Arline swung round and found herself looking into the grey eyes of her rescuer.

"Yes," she said at last, "I thought I might find him here."

"He went home ten minutes ago," Shandon explained. "At least, he left me ten minutes ago," he amended with a friendly smile.

"I expect he went over the back road," Arline said. "He often goes home that way from the pier. Did you manage to get the boat?"

He smiled down at her.

"Yes. We were able to bring her in intact, and we patched her up—all save the broken yard-arm, of course. I'm afraid your uncle will have to replace that later. Anyway, she is not much the worse for her adventure. She's moored to the quay over there."

He moved towards the old quay, and they sat on the broad sea-wall and looked down on the boat with its broken yard and brown sail lying in the bottom.

Arline turned to the man beside her.

"How can I ever thank you for all you have done—going out for the boat and fixing it up for us? You have been so kind. . . ."

He was looking down at her intently, and his grey eyes were grave for a moment.

"I hope there was no trouble when you arrived home?" he asked.

Arline evaded a direct answer.

"Oh, Uncle Henry was quite pacified when he discovered that he had not lost the boat altogether."

"I mean—about yesterday."

He was forcing her to reply.

"Not any more than I had expected."

She saw his lips draw together in a grim line.

"And that?" he questioned.

Arline looked away from his searching gaze.

"Need we go into—details?"

He shrugged almost indifferently.

"You have suffered no ill effects from the adventure, then?"

The tension was over, and Arline replied with a little rush of relief:

"No—none whatever. And you?"

He smiled down at her.

"Physically intact," he admitted.

"I don't suppose I shall ever be able to repay you," she said.

"Why not?" he replied. "You can always try, you know."

His tone was light again, and she met it thankfully.

"Oh—how?"

"Well——" He paused to consider her deliberately. "I am rather partial to a little encouragement," he admitted, "and you know I'm racing on Saturday afternoon."

"You mean, you would like me to come to the regatta and—cheer you on to victory?" Arline laughed.

"Why not?" he asked.

A little thrill of warmth went through her as she met his eyes.

"Will you come?" he asked at last.

"Yes—if you really want me to."

"I would hardly have asked you to come if I did not want you," he reminded her.

"Where must I stand?" she asked.

"Away from the crowd—so that I can see you and know that you are cheering for me."

"Would the Old Owl rock do?" she asked, entering into the spirit of his mood.

"Admirably. Then I can count on you?"

"Till you pass the winning mark."

"And after that?"

She hesitated.

"When you have won you won't need me to cheer you on," she laughed.

"I may need you to help me celebrate, though," he pointed out.

"I can hardly refuse," Arline declared. "I am so heavily in your debt."

"Then, the *Ganta* sails to victory on Saturday," he predicted, with the zest of a schoolboy.

"The *Ganta*," Arline mused. "I seem to have heard that name before."

"I may have mentioned it to you yesterday," he suggested.

"The memory seems to go further back than that—I'm sure," Arline persisted.

"Perhaps you've seen her lying in the bay over there."

He made a vague gesture towards Solan Point, where a racing craft had been moored beside the graceful length of the McCallum-Blairs' big yacht.

"You mean—that she belongs to—to——"

"To the people at Dunsolan House—to the McCallum-Blairs," he told her.

"Oh!"

Arline knew that she was staring at him with frank incredulity in her eyes. This thing was impossible. Gavin Shandon employed by the McCallum-Blairs. It was fantastic. Impossible!

Her recent stormy interview with her aunt came back to her vividly, and she remembered all that Mrs. Penner had had to say about the incident on the island, and how obviously anxious she was to keep the knowledge of it from the McCallum-Blairs. And now Gavin Shandon was telling her quite calmly that he was sailing the McCallum-Blair's yacht at the regatta. He was in the employ of the very people whom her aunt was determined should never hear of their unfortunate adventure.

"Is there anything wrong?" Shandon asked.

Arline pulled herself together with an effort.

"No—no, nothing. I was only rather—surprised about —the McCallum-Blairs."

"You know them, then?" he asked.

"No, I've never met them personally, but I believe my aunt has met Mrs. McCallum-Blair at the Ladies' Club."

"Does that make a difference to you standing on the Old Owl rock on Saturday and cheering for me?"

47

He asked the question with a whimsical smile that made his face seem almost boyish for a moment.

"Of course not," Arline replied promptly. "I'll be there if we stay for the regatta."

"Oh, you may be leaving Glen Solan, then?" he asked, with a hint of disappointment in his voice.

Arline avoided his direct gaze.

"Yes, we'll be leaving almost immediately."

"But I understood your cousin to say this afternoon that you might be here for the remainder of the summer," he said.

"Yes, that was my aunt's original intention, but—but she has changed her mind."

Suddenly he was looking at her intently, and the direct regard drew her eyes back to his face in spite of herself.

"Since this morning, I suppose?" he asked quietly.

She did not answer, but somehow she knew that he had guessed the truth. The grim expression had come back into his face, and his eyes were no longer smiling.

"I see," he said abruptly, and rose from his seat on the wall.

Arline slipped down from her perch and stood rather shyly before him.

"I must go now," she said, "but I promise to be there on Saturday."

She held out her hand in a little friendly gesture and he took it, holding it a moment while he said good-bye.

CHAPTER THREE

THE REGATTA

I

SATURDAY dawned bright and clear, with just sufficient breeze blowing to delight the hearts of the yachtsmen and keep the spectators cool and comfortable.

Arline had spent the previous day in a vain effort to please her aunt, but Mrs. Penner was in no mood to be reconciled. She had met each attempt at friendliness with an icy rebuff which had chilled her niece to the heart. At last Arline had given up trying, and had turned to her secretarial work, thankful beyond measure that there was plenty to keep her busy most of the day.

On Saturday morning, however, she rose with the delightful anticipation of an enjoyable day. Douglas, already attired in his immaculate white flannels, though it was still many hours before the first race, was in the morning-room when she went downstairs.

"Morning, Arline," he greeted her. "All set for the big day?"

"Yes," Arline replied. "I can see you are, too."

"How do you like the new blazer?" he asked.

"Very well indeed. You look fine."

"It may be a trifle bright at the moment," he commented, "but it will tone down in time."

"I see the *Commodore* is in the bay," Arline remarked. "I noticed it from my bedroom window."

"Yes, there's quite a stir already," Douglas admitted. "The Dunsolan yacht has steam up, too."

Arline turned sharply.

"Steam up? But—but, Dougie, I thought the McCallum-Blairs were away?"

"They may have been, but I guess they're back now," Douglas replied. "Old man McCallum-Blair wouldn't miss the first regatta of the season."

Mrs. Penner and Helen entered together, and after the first frigid greeting Mrs. Penner took little notice of her niece.

"We must start breakfast without your father," she said to Douglas. "He has overslept this morning, I'm afraid."

"Has he given Menzies the instructions about the yacht?" Douglas asked eagerly.

"I'm sure I can't say," Mrs. Penner replied. "I never interfere with your father's orders to the outside staff, as you know."

"But we *are* going to take her out?" Douglas questioned.

"Naturally." Mrs. Penner helped herself to another rasher of bacon, and surveyed her son critically. "I am still of the opinion that your blazer is just a trifle—loud, Douglas," she remarked. "Don't you think navy blue would have been more suitable?"

"More conservative, perhaps," Douglas replied, "but, never mind, this will soon tone down. I was just remarking that to Arline when you came in."

The observation seemed to draw his mother's attention to Arline for the first time since they sat down to the meal.

"And what do you propose to do this afternoon, Arline?" she asked frigidly.

In spite of the fact that she was not anxious to join the party in her uncle's yacht, Arline was a little hurt that it had been taken for granted that she should not accompany them.

"Well," she said a little distantly, "I thought of watching the regatta from somewhere along the shore."

"But, good heavens," Douglas protested, "what's the sense in that when we're taking the yacht? You'll get next to no view from the shore."

"I would much rather, all the same, Dougie," Arline replied truthfully.

"If Arline wants to stay behind there's no reason why we should try to force her to go with us," Mrs. Penner put in quickly.

Douglas glanced from his mother to his cousin, and something in the swift look which Arline shot at him kept him from protesting further.

"Oh, well, just as you like," he said kindly.

When Mr. Penner came downstairs it was arranged that they should have lunch half an hour earlier than usual, and get down to the yacht in good time. Henry Penner, in spite of his annoyance over the small boat, was surprised when he heard that Arline was not to join them in the yacht, but one look at his wife's face was sufficient to keep him from making any comment on the fact.

Helen, looking more frail and lovely than ever in a white silk frock and navy blue jacket, with white and navy shoes to match, was down in the hall before the others.

"I *do* wish you were coming with us," she said wistfully, when she saw Arline seated on the leather settee waiting to see them off. "There won't be very much fun for me without you."

"Nonsense," Arline laughed. "Look at the hosts of people you'll meet afterwards."

"I don't know that I want to meet hosts of people," Helen replied with a sigh.

"Of course you do. It will be loads of fun," Arline assured her.

"What will you do all the time?" Helen asked.

"Oh, watch the racing"—airily.

"But, I mean—afterwards?"

Arline smiled, and put an arm affectionately about her cousin's shoulders.

"Perhaps I will be able to tell you that much better to-night," she said.

"You mean, you're going to meet someone?"—eagerly.

"I hope so!"

"Oh, I'm so glad you won't be on your own. Is it— is it . . . ?"

"To-night, inquisitive one! Not a word of confession before to-night."

"All right," Helen laughed, "I won't ask any more questions! Oh, here's mother."

Mrs. Penner, in white linen from head to foot, came downstairs, with her husband, breathing heavily, in her wake.

"Well, come along, there's no need to stand about now we're all ready," Henry Penner said testily, adjusting his belt to a more comfortable notch as soon as his wife's back was turned. "Menzies will be waiting to get away. We'll have to look sharp, you know, if we want a good position."

51

He bustled past Arline with an elaborate pretence at not having noticed her and the fact that she was not dressed to accompany them.

"I've told Alice and cook that they can have the remainder of the day to themselves," Mrs. Penner remarked to Arline as they moved down the hall. "If you want anything to eat when you get back, tell them to arrange something cold for you."

"You won't be back to dinner then?" Arline asked.

"No. There's to be something at the Yacht Club. We'll stay for that, of course," Mrs. Penner said.

Helen slipped a warm hand into her cousin's as she passed, and gave it a little friendly clasp.

"Have a good time," she whispered.

Arline watched them until they had disappeared round the bend, and then went slowly upstairs to her own room to dress. She had plenty of time: the first race was not until two-thirty, and she knew that she would not be able to see Gavin Shandon before that, however much she desired to do so.

It was a queer twist of fate, she mused, that he should be in the employ of the McCallum-Blairs, but she had already decided that this fact should make no difference to their acquaintance. After all, she told herself, with a half smile, she was beginning to consider herself as someone in the employ of her aunt.

She caught a bus at the foot of the brae which took her to Solan Point, and from there she walked the remaining distance to the stretch of sand where the Old Owl sat with his feet in the water. It was a strangely shaped piece of rock, closely resembling an owl in formation, and some local artist had completed the illusion by painting in wings and two huge, saucer eyes. The paintwork was renewed every year, and the rock was a popular rendezvous for children of all ages.

To-day, however, the small stretch of sand was practically deserted, and Arline found a seat on a high ledge of rock with a clear view over the Firth. Soon she was busy picking out the boats she knew: the *Commodore;* her uncle's white yacht, the *Merrimae;* the graceful white curves of the McCallum-Blairs' steam yacht with its squat yellow funnel, and behind it, a trim little racing craft which she knew was the *Ganta*. Without a pair of glasses she was unable to see anything of what was going on on board the racing craft, but soon the first signal gun went off, and the boats began to jockey for position. When the second shot went off Arline's eyes were glued on the *Ganta's* scarlet length as she glided forward, effortless, beautiful, like a white-winged bird just poised on the crest of the waves and ready to take flight.

Although she knew very little of racing technique, it was obvious that the race was *Ganta's* from the start, yet there was all the excitement necessary to stimulate her interest in the very fact that Gavin Shandon's firm hand was on the tiller and that he had been anxious to win. She found herself on her feet waving her scarf above her head, as the scarlet and white line of the yacht turned the last buoy and sailed triumphantly past the winning flag.

It was easy to imagine Shandon's pleasure, and she pictured him, a quiet smile in his grey eyes, receiving McCallum-Blair's thanks. From what she had seen of Mr. McCallum-Blair, Arline imagined that he would be a very fine man to work for, and she began to tell herself that she was quite glad, after all, that Shandon was employed by McCallum-Blair. Surely a man like Mr. McCallum-Blair would not take Mrs. Penner's attitude towards the island incident. But what of Mrs. McCallum-Blair?

The thought pulled Arline up abruptly. Her aunt had said that Mrs. McCallum-Blair hated scandal, and if the incident on the island were presented to her in that light, might she not influence her husband to dispense with Gavin Shandon's services altogether? Arline wondered how hard it would be for him to find another position, and blamed herself afresh for ever having yielded to the temptation of taking her uncle's boat out of the bay.

She lay back on the grassy crown of the boulder which she had chosen as her grandstand, and looked up to the cloud-flecked canopy of sky above her. It was glorious to lie and think like this—pleasant thoughts—with no worry about passing time, she reflected, and let her mind slip into more cheerful channels.

"A penny for them—or are they worth much more than that?"

She started up to find Gavin Shandon standing on the sand beneath her looking up at her with a friendly smile in his grey eyes.

"My thoughts?" she replied gaily. "No—they weren't worth even a penny!"

"Disgraceful—on a day like this!"

He vaulted easily on to the rock and sat down beside her.

He was dressed in immaculate white flannels and a blue reefer jacket, with the peak of his yachting cap drawn down slightly over one eye. It was the first time Arline had seen him in a hat, and the rakish angle of the white cap gave him a rather dashing appearance that was quite disconcerting. She knew that he had changed since he had steered the *Ganta* to victory, and she admired the formal yachting rig-out, but somewhere deep within her was a rather wistful memory of a pair of old trousers and a sweater that was badly in need of attention at the elbows.

"I didn't expect you so soon," she told him.

"Why not?" he asked. "I said I would come as soon as the race was over."

"Yes, I know," Arline smiled, "but when I saw that the *Ganta* had won, I thought you might have to stay for a little while to—to celebrate the victory."

He lay back on the grass and looked up at her lazily.

"I understood you to say on Thursday that you were quite willing to celebrate with me," he reminded her.

"Yes—but . . ."

He sat up and took her hand firmly in his.

"What objections are there now, Arline?"

She wondered how he had discovered her name, but she did not think it strange that he should use it.

"None," she admitted after a moment.

He rose, still holding her hand, and pulled her to her feet.

"Then, shall we go?"

He led the way back over the stretch of sand towards the road.

"I'm afraid I haven't mapped out a very definite programme for the evening," he said. "I thought I would leave it to you to choose. There's a dance—quite an informal little affair—at the Yacht Club after dinner, or we could go into Oban if you like."

"If you don't mind, I'd—rather go to Oban."

54

"To be absolutely truthful, so would I," Shandon replied, as he helped her over the scattered rocks and they came out at last on the narrow coast road.

A small sports car was drawn into the side, and he approached it and flung his cap into the driver's seat. When his eyes met Arline's interrogatory glance there was a twinkle in their grey depths.

"I half expected you to choose the run to Oban, you see," he explained, "so I borrowed this for the occasion. I thought it might be more comfortable than the bus."

"Oh!"

Arline did not know quite what to say at this unexpected pleasure.

"Shall we keep to the coast, or would you like to take the road that goes by Loch Awe?" he asked, as he let in the clutch.

"Could we go by the coast, if you don't mind?" Arline asked. "I love the sudden glimpses of sea you get that way, and the fresh wind that always seems to be blowing in from the Firth."

"Your wishes are my commands to-day," he declared lightly. "We can always go by Loch Awe another time."

II

The sun was pouring down on Oban's blue bay and dappling the tree-clad hills above the town with patches of light and shade when Gavin brought the little car to a standstill in the garage he had chosen near the old harbour.

"We must have some tea right away," he declared. "I'm sure you must be parched after that ride in the hot sun."

"It was glorious!" Arline smiled. "I enjoyed every moment of it."

"I'm glad," he replied more gravely. "I want you to enjoy yourself, Arline."

"How did you find out my name?" she asked lightly, as he guided her towards an hotel on the Esplanade.

"Quite simple, my dear Watson. I merely asked the redoubtable Dougie."

"Oh—I see," Arline laughed.

"You have no objections?" he asked.

They were going up the broad white steps of the hotel, and heads were turned discreetly on the veranda lounge to watch them.

"None," Arline said, lowering her voice.

Tea was a delightful meal, served for them in one of the deep bay windows which overlooked the promenade and the vivid blue water beyond. They lingered quite a while in their secluded little alcove, while Shandon talked with great enthusiasm of yachting and the race he had won that afternoon. Arline thought that it must be very nice to feel so enthusiastic about one's job. It must make life so much easier, so much more pleasant.

"Well, shall we go now?" Shandon asked.

They walked slowly back towards the pier, watching the boats in the harbour and the sea-gulls circling overhead.

"It's one of the loveliest bays I've ever seen," Arline said, looking out to the long green slope of Kerrera lying peacefully under the sun.

"Yes. Oban has always the air of a Mediterranean port to me," Shandon said. "Have you ever seen the bay from McCaig's Folly?"

"No," Arline admitted. "It must be a wonderful view, though. I could never persuade anyone in the family to climb so far with me."

Shandon glanced at his wrist watch.

"We could do it easily before dinner," he suggested.

"Oh, I would love that," Arline cried.

"Then, it's settled. Come along."

All the austerity of the island encounter had left him, and Arline felt that she liked him even better in this gay mood. As they went up the steep incline together, hand in hand because some of the way was very rough, she felt that she could find a very true and worthwhile friend in Gavin Shandon.

This day was proving a perfect one to her. There was only one small cloud on Arline's new horizon—the fact that Shandon was doing his entertaining in a rather grand and, for him, expensive scale. They could so easily have gone to a little café for their tea, and now he was suggesting that they should return to the same hotel for dinner. She wondered if she could find a tactful way of suggesting a modest little supper somewhere to end up their day, instead of the dinner.

They were almost at the top of the narrow road which led to McCaig's Folly, and Shandon paused to help her up the last few steps. She was rather breathless when they reached the great circle of stone arches, and Shandon led her over to one which overlooked the bay.

Oban lay at their feet like a miniature town, with its white buildings sparkling in the sunshine. The boats in the harbour were like toys set in neat rows, and the green isle of Kerrera lay like some beautiful jewel in a sea of deepest aquamarine. Beyond the Firth of Lorne the hills of Mull rose up, benign giants watching over Glen More.

Arline drew in a deep breath.

"I'll never forget this—as long as I live," she said huskily.

Shandon, who was standing a little way behind her, did not reply, but there was a strange look in his grey eyes as he gazed out over the bay to the green slopes of Kerrera and remembered another island.

They sat down on a fallen block of stone and watched the changing panorama of the bay like a picture set in the dark frame of the stone arch.

"Well," Shandon said at last, "hadn't we better go down and get something to eat? You should be hungry by now."

Arline got to her feet, but she did not move away from the arch. It was going to be very difficult to broach the subject of dinner, and she knew that she ran the risk of arousing his anger once more, but she felt that she must protest now, or not at all.

"Mr. Shandon, need we go back—to the hotel, I mean? Couldn't we wait until later on and—and just have a little supper somewhere—in a café, where it's quieter and—and . . ."

She was blundering badly, she knew, and she dare not look at him. Yet, had she done so in that first moment, she would have seen that Gavin Shandon's expression was very far from one of anger. He knew why she had made the stumbling little suggestion, and when she met his eyes at last something that still lingered in their depths told her that he understood. However, he put his hand under her elbow in the now-familiar gesture which had in it an infinite suggestion of protection, and guided her over the rough ground to the road.

"Now, Arline, this is my day, and you know that you promised to help me celebrate!" he said firmly.

"Yes, I know, but . . ."

"Then, leave it to me," he smiled down at her, "and I promise I will be—discreet."

She found herself laughing with him again, her doubt dispelled, and realised that she could be ideally happy in his company.

The hotel lounge was crowded when they got back, but Shandon had obviously booked a table for dinner when they had taken tea there in the afternoon, and a waiter led them to a secluded corner of the great dining-room. Many of the diners were in yachting clothes and had come in from the regatta at Loch Solan. Arline glanced round for a familiar face in the gay throng, but could not see anyone whom she recognised. Shandon, however, seemed to be quite well known, and was constantly recognising the occupants of surrounding tables. Over their coffee, he pointed out a famous international yachtsman to her.

Arline's cheeks were flushed and her eyes very bright in the glow from the little crystal lamp as she looked across the table at him.

"Well, where now?" he asked.

"Oh! Isn't it almost time to go home?" she asked, a first note of regret tempering the gaiety of her voice.

He glanced down at his watch.

"It's only nine o'clock," he said. "We've time to run out as far as Ganavan—if you'd like that?" he added quickly.

Arline had often heard of the beauty of Ganavan Sands, but she had never had the opportunity of visiting them, and her eagerness to do so now put all thought of their return to Glen Solan from her mind.

"I'd love to go," she answered.

As they wound along the coast Arline lapsed into silence: the beauty all around her was too wonderful to express in speech, and she felt that her companion would understand her silence, would share in her love and appreciation of the vast stillness all around them.

As they drew up at Ganavan a solitary bird flew in from the sea, and its plaintive complaining cry echoed strangely in the night air, seeming to leave the little cove more still and quiet with its passing. A tiny bat brushed swiftly across the low windscreen in front of them and, with a little involuntary shiver, Arline drew nearer to her companion.

His arm was flung across the back of the seat and suddenly, she felt it slip to her shoulder and she was drawn into the circle of his embrace.

"Arline . . ." he murmured huskily, "you're very sweet. . . ."

His eyes were almost black as they looked down into hers in the gathering dusk and he caught her closer into his arms and pressed his lips to hers.

Arline lay back in his embrace, feeling that time had stopped and the world was very far away here in their sheltered cove. She gave herself up fully to that kiss, her hand straying at last to his dark hair and smoothing it gently against his head.

When she drew away a little, at last, she looked at him shyly, and he caught her to him again, though he did not touch her lips a second time.

It was the first great drops of rain which brought them back to full consciousness of their surroundings. Shandon glanced apprehensively at the sky.

"We'll have to make a move, I'm afraid," he said rather disappointedly.

She could not see his face clearly in the dim interior of the little vehicle as they spun swiftly along the narrow, winding road back to Oban. But the sweetness of his kiss still lingered for her, at least, and her eyes looked out dreamily at the shining daggers of light which the headlights made on the wet road. She knew that the beauty of Ganavan and the stillness of the quiet night that had hedged them round would remain with her, a shining, glorious memory, for all time. Nothing that the future might bring could ever take this one supreme moment from her now.

"I'm afraid it's going to be rather late before we get back," Shandon said, when they were approaching the first lights of the town. "Perhaps we should have gone straight back after dinner as you suggested."

There was a strange note in his deep voice, and Arline wondered if he were regretting the drive to Ganavan and that one brief kiss under the trees. She stole a glance at him in the dimness of the little car, but he did not turn to look at her. His eyes were fixed straight ahead as he set the car at a slower pace through the town.

Arline looked out of her window. The rain was very heavy now, pouring down on the pavements and filling the gutters. Groups of lightly clad people had taken shelter in most of the shop doorways, and the pavements were almost deserted.

"It's taken everyone unawares," Shandon remarked, as they approached the harbour. "I'm glad I had the car and that we were not forced to depend on the bus."

"We'd have missed it if we had waited as long as this," Arline smiled. "The last one goes out at ten o'clock."

"We'll be home before eleven," he said. "Will that be all right for you?"

"Oh, yes, I expect so," she replied.

As they passed the station two figures standing rather forlornly in the entrance caught her attention. There was something familiar about the floppy blue straw hat of the smaller of the two, and instantly she remembered Alice as she had stood in the hall at "Braeside" that afternoon, with the blue straw rigid in all the glory of its first appearance.

"Oh!" she exclaimed. "They've missed the bus."

Shandon turned towards her.

"Someone you know?" he asked, slowing down.

"Yes. Our cook and the parlourmaid. They came in for the evening, and they must have missed the last bus home to the Glen."

He turned the car round in a wide sweep.

"If they won't mind sitting in the back, I can offer them a lift," he volunteered.

"I'm sure they won't mind sitting anywhere as long as they get home," Arline replied. "It's awfully good of you."

"We can't very well leave them here, and it would be a longish walk for them," he smiled. "Can you open the door on your side?"

Arline pushed the door open as they drew up before the station entry.

"Alice—Nellie!" she called to the two girls.

Alice started, gazing through the rain at the car, but Nellie Anderson, a rather bold type of girl with big, blue eyes that always seemed just to avoid meeting a direct look, pulled the bewildered parlourmaid after her and hurried towards the car. She drew back a little when she recognised Arline.

"Oh—it's you, miss . . ."

But Alice almost fell into Arline's arms.

"Oh, miss, we've lost the bus. We didn't mean to wait so long, but the big picture was just finishin' an' the clock inside was slow."

"All right, Alice, accidents will happen," Arline said kindly. "Do you think you could manage to ride home in the back seat?"

"Oh, miss! It's so kind of you, miss," Alice cried, on the verge of tears.

Arline could not help thinking how quiet Gavin was during the drive back to Glen Solan, and contrasting his silence with the gay mood of the outward journey. She tried desperately not to admit, even to herself, that the change had taken place almost from the moment that he had bent his dark head and kissed her swiftly on the lips.

He spoke solely of trivialities, and sometimes he lapsed into silence for a long period. When he drew the car up at the foot of the brae at last, a quick glance at the little clock on the dashboard acquainted Arline with the fact that he had completed the journey in record time.

"There's no lights in the house," Alice said, heaving a quick sigh of relief. "Come on, Nellie. We'll be in first yet."

When the pair had disappeared round the bend of the drive, Arline turned to Shandon.

"I'm in your debt again," she said with a smile. "It was very good of you to give the girls a lift."

He seemed to recall his thoughts from a great distance.

"Oh, that," he said. "We could hardly have done otherwise, could we?"

He was smiling faintly, and her heart was suddenly light again.

"And now I'm afraid I must follow them," she said, holding out her hand. "I would like to be in before the family returns. I've had a wonderful day."

He took her hand and said very gently:

"You'll come again, Arline?"

"Yes," she whispered, almost too low for him to hear without bending his head.

"Perhaps I could even persuade you to let me show you how well the launch can perform when she has an adequate supply of petrol on board?"

There was a laugh in his voice, and she met it eagerly.

"If you promise to keep within safe distance of the mainland," she stipulated.

"Then, it's a promise," he said. "When? Monday morning?"

"At eleven o'clock," Arline replied. "And now, good night—and thank you again."

CHAPTER FOUR

CONFESSIONS

I

IT was after midnight when Arline heard the clang of the big iron gate which proclaimed the return of the rest of the family from the function at the Yacht Club.

The rain, which continued to fall, was pattering against her window pane, and she lay listening to the steady rhythm of it, while her thoughts slipped back over the events of the day.

The first light tap on her door passed unnoticed, so far away were her thoughts, and it was not until Helen appeared and called her softly by name that she became aware of her cousin.

"Helen, I thought you would have been much too tired to come," she whispered.

Helen glanced at the door to make sure that it was securely closed.

"Well, what happened?" she asked eagerly. "I had to come to find out all about it. Did you meet him, Arline?"

"Yes," Arline admitted. "I did."

Helen settled herself comfortably on the bed and clasped her arms round her knees.

"What did you do?" she asked. "Did you go anywhere exciting?"

"We went to Oban," Arline told her with a smile," and though we didn't do anything exciting, I enjoyed myself very much indeed."

There was something warm and friendly about Helen's presence there in the room, a note of the comradeship which Arline would have given a great deal to possess on many other occasions had Mrs. Penner permitted it. It made her joyous day seem more full to be discussing it like this with a sympathetic listener.

"I'm glad," Helen exclaimed. "Did you go to the pictures, or just for a walk?"

Arline smiled at her eagerness.

"We climbed up to McCaig's Folly and sat watching all the boats in the bay. It was beautiful. Have you ever been up at the Folly, Helen?"

Arline asked the question rather absentmindedly, and she was surprised at the look of confusion which spread over her cousin's face.

"Only once," Helen admitted, a deep colour staining her pale cheeks.

"Then you will know how marvellous the view is," Arline went on quickly, anxious to appear unconscious of the other's embarrassment. "We stayed there for quite a while, and then we came back and had something to eat at one of the hotels on the Esplanade. Afterwards," she continued, as Helen made no further remark, "we drove out to Ganavan Sands."

She drew in a deep breath at the memory of what had followed, but she knew that she could not even make Helen her confidant in the telling of that little scene. It would be locked in her heart for all time, a secret between herself and Gavin Shandon alone.

"And what did *you* do all day?" she asked.

Helen seemed to come out of a deep and not too happy reverie to answer the question.

"Oh, we stayed on the yacht and cruised about until all the races were over. Then we sat through the speech-making and the applause and the boring dinner at the Club."

"Helen," Arline laughed, "didn't you enjoy some part of the day?"

"Not one bit of it." Helen declared.

"Not even the dancing?"

"Well, the dance was quite nice, but I get so tired—so easily tired—and it was dreadfully stuffy in the club room because an old dowager was sitting by the window and insisted on it being kept shut. Then," Helen went on more slowly, "mother was rather annoyed."

"Oh!" Arline said, and almost added, 'what about this time?' but checked herself before the words were uttered.

"Yes. You see, the McCallum-Blairs were there," Helen replied.

"I should have thought that would have pleased Aunt Hilda."

"Oh, of course, it did," Helen admitted. "Mother was annoyed with me. You see, she thinks I didn't make myself nice enough to Mrs. McCallum-Blair."

"And did you?" Arline asked.

"I tried to," Helen said wearily, "but you know, Arline, when I meet people that I know I *must* be nice to I sort of dry up—go all queer inside and can't think of one single thing to say—one sensible thing, I mean."

Arline slipped a sympathetic hand into her cousin's.

"I know, Helen," she said, "I know exactly how you feel. I've been like that myself a dozen times, and generally ended up by saying the wrong thing."

"I don't think I even said the wrong thing," Helen confessed. "I just 'sat like a dummy,' as mother told me later, and said nothing."

"Has Mrs. McCallum-Blair that effect on one?" Arline asked.

"No, really she was quite charming," Helen defended wholeheartedly. "It was mother who confused me."

"Don't worry about it," Arline advised kindly. "I'm sure Aunt Hilda doesn't mean to be so—so upsetting."

"She wanted me to meet Mrs. McCallum-Blair's son, of course," Helen said hurriedly, as if she must get the information out as quickly as possible.

"And—did you meet him?"

Helen shook her head.

"That's another reason for mother's annoyance," she said. "He wasn't there."

Arline imagined for a moment that there was a faint gleam of relief in Helen's blue eyes as she made the revelation.

"Well, perhaps another time . . ." she suggested.

Helen turned swiftly on the bed as if the suggestion had stung her.

"I don't want to meet him!" she cried, her blue eyes misty with the tears of suppressed emotion. "I don't want to meet him, ever. I hate him! I hate all the scheming and plotting and intrigue that is going on here—the attempts to push me into his company or into the company of any other available eligible that may be around at the moment. I hate it all! I hate the fine clothes, and the yachts, and the talk of Cannes, and Biarritz and Switzerland. I hate it, I tell you! And more than everything, I hate myself."

Arline leaned over and put her arms protectively round the thin shoulders.

"Helen, dear! Helen—don't distress yourself so," she pleaded. "Try to tell me what's wrong."

Helen was quivering from head to foot, and her breath was coming gaspingly between her dry lips. She held on to Arline's hand as if it were the only concrete thing in a tottering world.

"I'll try," she breathed at last, "only have patience with me, Arline. . . ."

"All right, dear—all right," Arline soothed her.

At last Helen looked up and met her eyes quite frankly.

"I didn't mean to burst out like that," she said, still rather shakily. "I know you have plenty of things to worry you without me adding mine to them."

"You know 'a trouble shared is a trouble halved,' Helen," Arline began. "Besides, I may be able to help."

Helen shook her head.

"I don't think so, but I dare say I would have told you sooner or later, anyway!"

"You know you can always come to me," Arline assured her.

"Arline," Helen said slowly, as if she were speaking from some great distance, "have you ever loved anyone—solely, completely—so much so that it hurts?"

Arline looked at the pale face beside her and for a moment she did not know how to answer.

"No, Helen," she said at last, "I don't think I have."

Helen sighed.

"Perhaps you are lucky, then," she said wearily.

"You mean, you've found someone—fallen in love?"

Helen, responding to the ready sympathy in her cousin's voice, looked up and gave Arline a tremulous smile.

"Oh, I've wanted to tell you ever since—ever since it happened," she said with a rush, "but there never seems to be any time to talk quietly to one another."

"Is it someone I know?" Arline asked.

Helen shook her head.

"I met him at Beth Hendries' tennis party last summer. Someone had brought him along and then left him to look

66

after himself," she explained. "I think he felt out of it a little—you know what most of Beth's friends are like—and I did, too. I can never stand up to games; even tennis soon makes me tired. Well, we sat together and talked—and there was quite a lot we had in common."

"Where did you meet him again?" Arline prompted.

"I didn't—at least, not until the beginning of this year," Helen continued. "Then I met him quite by accident in Buchanan Street one day when I had been to the dressmaker's. I realised then that he had been in my thoughts almost daily since that first meeting at Beth's. And, Arline—there was something which told me that I had been very constantly in his."

"You still meet him, then?" Arline asked.

"Not very often," Helen replied wistfully. "Only when I can get away from mother."

"Can you understand what it's like for me always to have to meet him in secret, slyly, as if our love were something to be ashamed of?" she cried. "I can't even plan to meet him. We have to snatch our moments together; an hour in the Park before dinner while mother is resting—a hasty telephone call when there's nobody at home some mornings—brief glimpses of one another over a restaurant meal in Alex's lunch hour—always stolen moments, Arline, with the thought for ever at the back of my mind that I'm going to be found out."

"Why don't you tell Aunt Hilda?" Arline asked.

Helen gave a little, mirthless laugh.

"What do you think she would say?" she asked.

"After all, if you love—Alex. . . ."

"Love doesn't mean anything to mother! She just wouldn't—*couldn't* understand how anyone with all the 'advantages' that I have been given in life could be so ungrateful as to fall in love with a shop assistant. Alex is a chemist, but that wouldn't mean a thing to mother. That he works in a shop—and not his own shop at that—would be enough."

Arline could see the situation so plainly. From her own intimate knowledge of Mrs. Penner she could feel all the thwarted hope that poor Helen must have felt a hundred times in the silence of her lonely room. She only wished that her cousin had given her her confidence earlier. There might have been ways in which she could have helped a little.

"Sometimes I've felt terrible when I've had to tell a lie about where I've been," Helen went on. "Not because of mother, but because lying and—Alex are so far apart. He's so fine, Arline. I wish you could meet him. The other day when I went away to Oban in the car by myself I felt dreadfully mean not asking you to come, but mother was so—displeased, and Alex was coming up for the day to Oban. It was my only chance, and I hadn't seen him for so long."

Arline had almost forgotten the incident of Helen's speedy departure for Oban, but now she remembered how confused her cousin had looked as she drove off alone.

"That doesn't matter, Helen," she assured her quickly. "I only wish I could help you in some way. Are you sure it would be no use approaching Aunt Hilda?"

She knew that her suggestion was a forlorn hope even before Helen shook her head.

"Perhaps if she met Alex . . .?"

"I'm afraid it wouldn't make any difference," Helen said, with a sigh which held resignation. "Mother has made up her mind that I must marry into a 'good' family— preferably the McCallum-Blairs of Dunsolan."

"But you haven't even met the man," Arline objected fiercely. "He may be—anything."

"As long as he's Mrs. McCallum-Blair's son that's good enough for mother. Oh, Arline—sometimes I wish it were all over and—and I *knew* that Alex and I—would never have each other. . . ."

"Don't talk like that, dear," Arline urged. "Surely it's worth putting up a fight for—that sort of love?"

Helen gave a faint sigh and slipped from the bed.

"I can't, Arline," she whispered. "What would be the use? It's always the same in the end. Mother always wins."

"But, Helen," Arline protested, but Helen bent down suddenly and kissed her on the cheek.

"Don't worry about me, Arline," she said huskily. "I know it will all have to end sometime, but, just now, it's so beautiful that sometimes there isn't even room for doubts and fears."

She was gone with that, tiptoeing down to her room so that she might not awaken her mother.

Arline switched off the light above her bed and lay very still in the darkness. The intimate presence of the night had left her, and the place was alive with shadows. Her heart began to beat suffocatingly close to her throat, and for one wild moment she knew fear—fear for Helen.

The feeling was gone in an instant, but the clock in the hall downstairs had chimed two before she fell asleep.

II

Sunday was the only day at "Braeside" when Arline could consider herself completely at liberty, and that, probably, because there was no post to attend to and no collection from the two pillar-boxes in the village. It had become a habit with her to take a short walk on the hillside immediately behind the house after breakfast. Sometimes Helen would join her, but more often it was Douglas who fell into step with her on the narrow path that climbed on to the moor.

This morning, however, Mrs. Penner had called Helen to her room, and Douglas was nowhere to be seen when Arline went through the kitchen garden to the wicket gate which led directly on to the hill.

It was a glorious day, with the trees and the grass washed a fresher green by the rain of the night before, and the sky quite guiltless of cloud. Arline walked quickly: there was a freshness about the morning that made her even want to run. She skirted the dark belt of trees which crowned the hill and, when she was safely out of sight of the house, gave way to her desire, and ran down the next grassy slope in the face of the wind. Almost at the bottom she was pulled up by the sharp, staccato bark of a dog following at her heels. As she slowed down, a small Scotch terrier romped past her, his short legs almost hidden in the long grass. He wheeled round quickly and came charging back, full of enthusiasm, his small stump of a tail wagging vigorously.

"Hullo, boy!" Arline greeted him, and stooped to pat him.

The first impression she had of the dog's owner was of two bare, brown legs thrust into white sandals and a swinging kilt as a girl came running down the slope in their wake.

"I'm so sorry," she said breathlessly, "I couldn't stop him, but he won't harm you. He's very friendly."

"So I see," Arline answered, looking into the hazel eyes of the girl before her. "I expect he was feeling the same way about the morning as I was when I started to run."

"Isn't it glorious," the girl replied enthusiastically, stretching her arms high above her head as if to embrace the beauty of the new day. "I love to be out early like this, don't you?"

"Yes, I do."

The girl would be about fourteen, Arline thought, but there was nothing of the gauche schoolgirl about her. She had a straightforward, simple manner that was wholly delightful, and when she laughed her red lips parted to show two rows of even, spaced teeth that gleamed like pearls.

"I love a walk so early in the day," she said, "and Jock has come to expect it now. If I don't start out immediately after breakfast he barks so loudly that he becomes quite a nuisance."

"A most sensible dog," Arline smiled. "He certainly knows what's good for him."

They were walking on down the hill, and the girl said:

"I hope you don't mind me coming along with you?"

Arline assured her that she thought it a delightful thing to have company on such a morning.

"I do, too," the girl replied. "I'm afraid I can't interest anyone at home in my early-morning rambles—anyone other than Jock, of course," she added, looking after the little terrier with one of her swift smiles.

"Do you often come to the hill in the mornings?" Arline asked conversationally.

"Every morning—except Sunday, as a rule, but to-day mother didn't feel like going to church, and, as she was staying in bed with a slight headache, and Jock was making a terrible noise, I thought I had better take him out of the way." She turned to look at Arline. "Do you come often? It's strange that we haven't met before this."

"It isn't really strange when you consider that I *only* come on Sunday mornings and you come every day except Sunday," Arline smiled.

"Oh, I see," her companion said. She studied Arline for a moment as they swung down the hill path together. "You know," she said at last, "I'm rather sorry about that."

"I believe I am, too," Arline confessed, as they passed through the turnstile.

The girl turned to whistle for her dog who had gone off with a scurry of short black legs and an eager nose in the direction of the wood.

"Jock simply loves chasing rabbits," she called back to Arline over her shoulder, "and he really mustn't."

"Are you anxious about the rabbits?" Arline asked.

"I'm not," the girl laughed. "Jock would never catch a rabbit in a hundred years! No, I'm anxious about him. He's got a terrible habit of forgetting that there's anyone with him when he's rabbit-hunting, and it sometimes takes me quite a while to find him. Then, of course, we're late for something—generally a meal. It's no use scolding Jock, of course."

Arline followed her towards the wood, where they found the miscreant doing his best to enlarge a rabbit burrow in the side of a low bank. The girl sat down beside her pet and rolled him over playfully on the long grass.

"Jock! you bad dog. How many times have I to tell you that rabbits are positively forbidden," she reprimanded.

"And on Sunday morning, too!" Arline put in, seating herself on the grass beside Jock's mistress.

The girl laughed and stretched out on the grass, her hands clasped loosely behind her smooth dark hair. Arline, feeling curiously at peace, looked around her. The bank on which they sat was crowned by a group of rhododendron bushes just bursting into flower. Deep purple and white alternating, they were a brilliant splash of colour against the darker green heart of the wood.

"How beautiful they are!"

The girl jumped up with the graceful movement which Arline had noticed several times during their short encounter, and climbed up the bank to pull down a bunch of blossom which had burst fully into flower. She returned

71

with it to the bank and swept Arline a deep curtsy, placing the flowers in her lap with a smile.

"For you," she said.

"How nice," Arline cried, "and how beautifully you did that! Do you dance?"

"However did you guess?" her companion smiled.

"Oh," Arline said lightly, "from the curtsy and the way you offered the flowers."

The girl knelt down on the grass before her and ran her slim brown hands in a little caressing gesture over the green turf. Her eyes were full of a soft light, the eager glow of enthusiasm.

"Yes," she said slowly, "I've been dancing ever since I can remember. I love it. It's part of me, the only part of my life that I *know* I'll go on enjoying for all time."

"You mean to take it up professionally, then?"

There was a long pause in which the girl gazed out over the undulating slopes of the hills as if she would read her future there. At last, she shook her head.

"I don't know. No, I don't think so."

"Oh, but isn't that rather a pity?" Arline said quickly. The clear hazel eyes looked up at her immediately.

"It is," the girl said unhesitatingly, "because, you see, I love it, and I know I could make such a success of it!"

It was the calm statement of a person who was sure beyond any shadow of doubt in which direction her one talent lay.

"I live for the winter months when I can go back to my dancing lessons!" the girl went on dreamily. "We live in Glasgow most of the time, and I have my lessons there. I'm a pupil of Kay Lang's. When I was younger," she continued, "mother rather encouraged the idea. She let me have a practice room at home, with a bar and mirrors fitted up for the ballet exercises, but I'm afraid she thinks I am considering it too seriously now."

"Perhaps you can persuade her to take your view when you tell her how very fond you are of it," Arline suggested.

"Oh, I *do* hope I can," the girl said, with a wistful smile. "I'm afraid, though, it's going to make her very disappointed in me. I don't think mother ever really cared for the idea after I was about twelve. She hoped I would

72

grow out of it, as most of the others who go to the classes do. They don't really take it seriously, I'm afraid."

At this moment Jock came trotting back and stood on the road at the foot of the bank, head on one side, his short stump of a tail wagging energetically.

"It's Jock's turn to remind *me* that we should be moving," the girl said, getting to her feet and shaking out the folds of her kilt.

Arline got up and turned towards the stile.

"I must go back this way," she explained. "I live on the hill, you see."

The girl held out her hand.

"I'm so glad we met," she said, with a frank smile. "I hope we are going to see each other again—quite soon." She was leaning against the stile through which Arline had passed, and she continued quickly: "Would you tell me your name, please? I should so much like to know it."

Arline smiled at this friendly overture, replying promptly enough:

"Arline Hamilton."

"Oh!" The girl smiled frankly up at her. "It's a very nice name. Mine is Sheena McCallum-Blair. Some day we might meet again. Good-bye, Miss Hamilton."

She was gone, her kilt swinging as she went down over the grassy road, the little black dog trotting contentedly by her side. Arline stood watching her as she went, her hands gripping the top bar of the wooden stile.

Sheena McCallum-Blair? Sheena McCallum-Blair! Was her young and delightful companion of the hillside Mrs. McCallum-Blair's daughter?

III

When Arline turned in at the little wicket gate she was surprised to see the big Daimler drawn up outside the garage doors. She approached swiftly and met Douglas coming out of the garage with a spare tin of petrol in either hand.

"Had a nice walk?" he asked.

"Yes, Dougie, splendid," Arline replied, coming down the few steps to the flagged courtyard. "I met such an

73

interesting girl on the hill, too. She was out exercising her dog and we walked as far the the High Wood together. Look! The rhododendrons are out already."

She still carried the spray of blossom Sheena McCallum-Blair had picked for her, and she held it up for her cousin to admire.

"It looks as if it's pretty useless to make friends here," he said slowly.

"Dougie, what's happening? Are we . . .?"

Douglas glanced hastily away from the concern in her eyes.

"We're going home," he said bluntly, but not unkindly. He was at the age where he found no way of dressing up the truth, however unpleasant it might be.

"To Glasgow?"

"Yes."

"Why? Dougie, why?"

"Because Mother has suddenly and irrevocably made up her mind that we cannot stay in Glen Solan even half a day longer."

Even before she became fully aware that Douglas was struggling under deep embarrassment, Arline felt that this new and unexpected turn of events was in some way closely connected with herself. It was characteristic of her that she did not stop to question her cousin further, but went straight to the lounge where she knew she would find her aunt at that time in the morning.

Mrs. Penner was alone. She was seated in one of the deep velvet chairs near the window, an unopened periodical in her lap, while her long fingers drummed restlessly on the low wooden sill. She spoke without turning, and Arline realised that she had been taken for Helen.

"Has Arline come back yet? You remember that I want to see her immediately. *Immediately,* you understand, Helen."

Arline moved forward.

"You want to see me, Aunt Hilda?"

Mrs. Penner swung round in her chair.

"Oh, so you have returned!" She rose to her feet and advanced into the centre of the room. "Perhaps, if you have a moment to spare, you may explain where you have been to this time of day."

Gone was the air of martyrdom, gone was all pretence of frailty. Arline glanced at the clock under its glass case, fearing that her own wrist watch had betrayed her into returning late for lunch, but there was still about an hour to spare before the gong. She turned back to her aunt.

"I went for a short walk on the hill, Aunt Hilda," she explained. "I generally do on a Sunday morning."

Mrs. Penner's cloak of cold reserve seemed to slip from her at the words, and there was a gleam of definite antagonism in her blue eyes as she stepped across the room and closed the door which Arline had left ajar behind her.

"Who was your companion?" she demanded.

Arline hesitated for a bare fraction of a second in which she debated the advisability of mentioning Sheena Blair's name.

"I—met a girl on the hill," she said quietly. "We walked as far as the High Wood."

Mrs. Penner gave a short and peculiarly mirthless laugh which just escaped being a sneer.

"It's quite useless to evade the issue," she said. "I happen to know the truth.

Arline drew herself up with a little unconscious movement.

"Aunt Hilda, I have told you the truth."

Mrs. Penner's brow drew together.

"Perhaps about this morning," she replied sharply. "I have no proof otherwise, but I *do* know about last night, and, after all, that is the real issue."

Arline's clear eyes did not waver as they met the cold blue stare of her aunt's.

"You met that man again last night," Mrs. Penner continued, her anger beginning to struggle uppermost. "This is not the first time you have gone behind my back in such a—such a despicable way after I had warned you." She turned from the calm scrutiny of Arline's eyes and began to pace the room, not looking at her niece while she continued her tirade. "To think of all we have done for you, too, and this—*this* is how you return our generosity. To think that I must be humbled by my own servants. That I must be told of your disgraceful conduct through the medium of a domestic!"

Arline, who had been vainly trying to piece together the scraps of information which had caused her aunt's fresh displeasure, had a sudden vision of Alice and Nellie Anderson standing in the rain at the entrance to Oban Station, and Gavin Shandon's generous offer to drive them home. It was an easy mental step to link this little scene with her aunt's accusations, and Arline knew beyond doubt that Alice was not the guilty party. She remembered Nellie Anderson's sullen silence, and knew that the cook was an habitual tale bearer.

"You met him again," Mrs. Penner repeated sharply. "Surely you are not attempting to deny that?"

"I had no intention of denying anything, Aunt Hilda," Arline replied. "Yes, I met Mr. Shandon. I spent the evening in Oban with him after the regatta."

Her confession was calm and deliberate, and her head was held high in the gesture Mrs. Penner resented for no other reason than that it made her feel, somehow, in the wrong. However, she prided herself that she was never at a loss to deal with any situation, and drew herself up to renew the attack.

"You admit it quite calmly, I see. I might have been prepared for this," she continued, forcing the old resigned note into her voice. "Indeed, I believe I expected it. You have never had any respect for the proprieties—never! Not content with the disgraceful incident of last week, you join this man again immediately I turn my back."

"But, Aunt Hilda," Arline protested, "surely you can't object to a perfectly normal visit to Oban for the evening."

"Perfectly normal!" Mrs. Penner paused to laugh. "Perfectly normal! With your name and his on every gossip's tongue in the village. A common deck hand and my niece! And then you give them cause for further conjecture."

"Don't you think that perhaps this situation is not quite so—serious as that?" Arline put in. "I can't really see why there should be all this fuss because somebody saved my life. After all, I am old enough to choose my friends."

Mrs. Penner swung round in her restless pacing.

"While you remain under my roof, Arline, I will have some say in the matter of your choice of friends. Don't forget that *our* names are probably being linked with this disgraceful business, and I can't afford that sort of gossip to continue here. I must think of Helen. As it is, there has been enough damage done, and you can rest assured that I don't mean to remain here to see it completed by your persistent folly."

"You mean to go back to Glasgow, then?" Arline asked.

"Immediately!"

"Aunt Hilda, isn't that a rather drastic step?"

"Not as I see the situation!"

"What—exactly—is the situation?"

"I think I have gone into all this before," Mrs. Penner said, assuming an air of weariness. "I am determined that the friends I have made here will not hear of this gossip if I can help it—for Helen's sake and my own."

"Therefore, you mean to move completely away?"

"For the time being, until the incident is forgotten."

"There's no need for that, Aunt Hilda," Arline said quickly. "I mean, you can't penalise the whole family on my account. Dougie and Helen both love to be here. It isn't fair to them, really it isn't."

"It is quite evident that you are pleading your own case," Mrs. Penner interrupted, "but I'm afraid it's no use. My mind is made up—doubly so since the McCallum-Blairs are in residence at Dunsolan House again."

For a moment Arline felt that she hated the McCallum-Blairs. However, there were other things to think of just now—a broken-up holiday which she knew would be a great disappointment to Douglas, at least.

"Let me go back alone," she suggested, and even as she did so the thought of Gavin Shandon stabbed to her heart.

"Certainly not!" Mrs. Penner's smile was not pleasant to see. "If I can't trust you her under my very eyes, do you think I would be fool enough to let you go back to Glasgow alone?"

Arline flushed scarlet. It was very hard to keep an even temper under the circumstances.

"Very well," she said, turning towards the door, "I suppose there's nothing for it but to go back, but I'm sorry that you won't allow me to save the others' holiday by going alone."

"I believe the rest of my family are sensible enough to realise what is at stake, and they will not grumble."

Mrs. Penner's Parthian shot rang in Arline's ears as she ascended to her own room to change.

She had done nothing wrong, she convinced herself a dozen times, as she folded clothes into her old suitcase. And then she thought of Gavin Shandon and the promise she had made to meet him the following day.

It was useless to appeal to her aunt—to hope that Mrs. Penner would recognise the need for explanations. Yet she felt that she could not leave Glen Solan like this, without a word. She must communicate with Gavin somehow so that he might not wait for her in vain in the morning. But how was she going to find him?

The only thing to do was to write him a short, explanatory note, and hope that it would reach him safely. She could send it to the McCallum-Blairs' yacht, and it would be delivered in the morning before he set out to meet her.

She sat with her pen poised over the blank sheet for several minutes before she headed it "Braeside, Sunday."

With that effort, however, her imagination deserted her. Surely it was easy enough to pen a few lines of apology for a cancelled engagement, she thought, but two attempts were crushed and thrown into the waste-paper basket before she felt even remotely satisfied. She picked up the third sheet, and read over what she had written:

"Dear Mr. Shandon,

"Owing to unforeseen circumstances, we are leaving Glen Solan this afternoon. I hope you will forgive me for not keeping the appointment to-morrow morning and believe me when I say that I deeply regret not being able to do so.   "Yours very sincerely,
                                    Arline Hamilton."

It sounded curt, even unfriendly, she thought, and suddenly there were tears in her eyes as she pictured him reading it. What would he think? Would he believe that it was merely her way of ending a friendship that she had no further desire to keep?

She folded the single sheet of notepaper, sealed and addressed the envelope, and went slowly downstairs.

It was not until the Daimler had left Glen Solan far behind in the haze of that warm afternoon that Arline suddenly remembered that there was no collection from the village post-boxes on a Sunday.

CHAPTER FIVE

THE HOUSE ON THE CLYDE

I

IT had been one of the coldest Junes on record, and the sudden hot spell which followed in the first days of July filled the river steamers and the coast-bound trains to capacity, while the less fortunate inhabitants of Glasgow gravitated to the parks and open spaces to take full advantage of the sun.

Arline, walking the length of the Great Western Road, felt the heat of the pavements striking through the fine leather of her shoes, and turned in at the main gates of the Botanical Gardens, deciding to return to Westwood Drive by this more pleasant route.

It was almost a month since they had left Glen Solan. A month! And in that time she had found herself thinking constantly of the man who had come to her rescue that misty day on the Lorne Firth. Gavin Shandon!

In those first days after their departure from the Glen she had watched each post, half hoping that he would reply to her letter, yet knowing in her heart that he was ignorant of her Glasgow address. She had followed the newspaper reports of the yacht racing, and found *Ganta's* name among the winners in two Clyde regattas, during June. She wondered where Shandon was now, and if he ever thought of her. He was never very far from her own thoughts these days, she confessed inwardly, and Helen had asked once or twice if she had heard from him. Arline had left her in town that morning, and the eager light in her cousin's blue eyes had told her that Helen would take the opportunity of a snatched moment with Alex Framer.

Lingering at the far gate of the Gardens in the hope that she might catch Helen as she came off the tram at the terminus, Arline wondered how her cousin's romance would end, and meeting Helen's glowing eyes half an hour later, she prayed that there might only be happiness in store for this generous-hearted cousin of hers.

"It was perfectly sweet of you to wait for me!" Helen said, as she came up. "Have I kept you a disgraceful time?"

"No, I walked through the Gardens. It was lovely in there—shady and cool beside the river."

They turned into Westwood Drive and Arline lapsed into silence as they approached number five.

"I wonder if mother has gone down to the coast?" Helen said, stooping to open the gate. "If she has, there's just the chance that we might be able to have the car for the afternoon. I'm pining for a breath of fresh air after all this heat, aren't you?"

"Yes, it would be pleasant," Arline admitted, and added with a note of relief in her voice as she opened the front door and passed into the coolness of the hall: "I think Aunt Hilda has gone."

Alice, coming through from the dining-room, verified the fact that her mistress had left shortly after eleven o'clock. Douglas, Alice explained, had gone with his mother, and they were not expected back until dinner. Mr. Penner, she added, had gone to the Golf Club for the day.

Over their lunch the two girls discussed their plans for the afternoon.

"We can't go very far," Arline pointed out. "It's fairly late now."

"Let's stick a pin in the road map!" Helen suggested with unusual gaiety, "and then tell Coats to go there!"

While Helen ordered the car Arline found the road map and, with much solemn ceremony, stuck the pin in.

"It's as near Rowardennan as make no matter," Helen declared. "Actually, you've stuck it in Ben Lomond, but as we can't get a car up the Ben, you'll have to be satisfied with sticking to the road! I've never been up that side of the loch, have you?"

Arline shook her head.

"No, but I've always thought I'd like to go."

The car was at the front door when they came out and Coats, the chauffeur, was waiting.

"Go out the Drymen Road, Coats," Helen said. "You know the way?"

"Very well, miss. It should be nice out there to-day."

Arline sat back in the car with a sigh of relief. It was glorious to get away like this, and so seldom that she found herself alone with Helen these days.

They were running through the main road of Bearsden when Helen said rather abruptly:

"The McCallum-Blairs live here, you know."

"Oh!"

Arline sat up in her corner and looked about her. A school building rose on her right and they flashed past a short row of well-kept shops towards another residential area.

"I'm not quite sure where, of course," Helen went on, "but I remember mother mentioning the fact."

"It's rather a nice place," Arline replied, wondering whether she should tell Helen that Gavin Shandon was employed on the McCallum-Blairs' yacht or not.

They were through the village now and out in open country, with the wind blowing fresh and sweet across the moors and the Campsie Fells green and clear against the sky to the east. When they reached Balmaha, and the blue sweep of Loch Lomond lay before them with the scattered islands riding the clear waters like tiny green skiffs, she felt that life was very good indeed in some ways.

Coats was driving more slowly now, going along at a leisurely pace so that they might enjoy the view to the full. They left him to look after the car when they reached Rowardennan, and walked down beside the edge of the loch. It was narrow here, and the great hills on the Luss side came sweeping down into the water, making it look dark and still and mysterious.

Helen sat down on a smooth boulder on the shore and clasped her hands round her knees.

"How peaceful it is here, Arline," she said wistfully. "Why can't life be like this?"

"It's not life that's wrong," Arline said quickly. "It's people who *make* life all wrong sometimes."

"You think we can control our own destinies?" Helen asked doubtfully.

"To a very great extent."

"You mean that nine times out of ten it is our own fault if things go wrong?"

"Perhaps not quite such a high average, but frequently a lot of our so-called bad luck is due to some flaw in our own make-up."

"Such as—say, pride?" Helen asked, deeply interested.

"Yes, pride is as good an example as any. What blunders have been committed in the sacred name of pride!"

"What about pride—and love?" Helen asked suddenly. "That's a pride in a class by itself, isn't it? It's the most easily hurt pride; the sort of pride that strikes back blindly—a sort of wretched pride."

Arline lay back on the grass and half closed her eyes. Helen studied her idly for a moment and then said abruptly:

"Arline, have you heard from Gavin Shandon yet?"

Arline's dark lashes swept upwards.

"No," she said. "I didn't leave him my address."

"Oh, why not? I thought you—rather liked him?"

Arline smiled.

"I did rather like him," she admitted, "but we left the Glen in such a hurry."

The memory of Glen Solan and that last ride to Oban swept over her and stirred a thousand memories in her heart, memories that she had tried in vain to stifle in the past few eventless weeks.

"I'm so sorry everything turned out as it did," Helen said gently. "I wish we had stayed longer in the Glen."

Helen was being magnanimous. The fact that their return to Glasgow had given her a greater chance of seeing Alex more frequently hardly seemed to occur to her.

"Don't worry about it, Helen," Arline said, her eyes closed again so that her cousin might not see the shadow that lay in them. "It just can't be helped, I suppose."

"You'll meet him again—I feel sure of it," Helen declared. "Have you no idea which yacht he's with?"

Arline sat up.

"Yes," she said quietly. "He's on the *Ganta*."

"The *Ganta*?" Helen echoed. "The McCallum-Blair's yacht? Oh!" She could not disguise her astonishment.

"You see, it's rather awkward," Arline smiled a little forced smile.

"Does mother know?" Helen asked.

"No."

There was a moment's pause, then Helen said:

"I don't see that it matters at all whom he works for. You don't think it does, do you?"

"It doesn't make any difference to me."

"It *is* rather queer, though, isn't it?" Helen went on. "Of all the yachts he could have been on . . ."

"I suppose that's just life—as we said before."

Helen was more serious, however.

"You *do* want to see him again, though, don't you?" she asked.

"If he wants to see me."

"Well, you didn't leave him any address to write to, you know," Helen pointed out. "It's a dreadful muddle," she sighed, when Arline made no reply to her last remark. "It's queer how love can't just be smooth and straightforward when it comes. I suppose it would have been too much to ask of fate that Alex might have been Mrs. McCallum-Blair's son."

Arline laughed.

"Yes, I suppose that *would* be asking too much. What are you going to do about Alex, Helen?" she asked more seriously.

A deep colour stained Helen's cheeks.

"I don't know," she said slowly. "Sometimes I feel that I want to rush out and shout our love from the hill tops, and then I realise my weakness, and I know that I am afraid of mother. I hate myself for being so weak, but I can't help myself. I've grown up with the feeling. It's part of me now."

"Helen, don't you think fear might become part of your love, too?" Arline asked gently.

"I don't know." Helen's voice was strangely shaken. "Sometimes I feel that there is no hope, then something inside me *knows* that Alex and I will be together in the end—for all time." She turned towards her cousin, and Arline saw the strange glow that transformed her face. "It's worth all the pain and doubt to know that," she went on softly. "I wish I could tell you how I feel—so that you might feel it, too. It is as if the sun would break through the dark clouds, and all pain and misery would be swept away like—like mist across the hills."

Arline sat very still. She could find no adequate words with which to reply, and Helen's soft tones seemed to linger in the silence between them.

"And all pain and misery will be swept away like mist across the hills!"

II

Douglas was alone in the lounge when they arrived back at Westwood Drive with an hour to spare before dinner.

"Where's mother?" Helen asked.

"In her room, I expect, removing the stains of travel," Douglas answered briefly. "Where have you been? I see you had the car."

"It was so hot," Helen replied, taking off her gloves and tossing them on a side table. "We fancied a run, so Coats took us up as far as Loch Lomond."

"Very nice, I should imagine. I don't suppose you had a shot at climbing the Ben?" he laughed.

"No, we were very lazy," Arline explained, "and just sat on the shore and gossiped."

"It was glorious up there, Dougie," Helen said. "Everything's so quiet and fresh when you get up that far. Where did you go?"

Douglas glanced at the door which the girls had left open behind them.

"I don't know if it is a state secret until we are all gathered round the family board," he began, "but I'll tell you now in case the shock unsettles you later and you can't do justice to the meal."

"Well, go on. What is it?" Helen demanded.

"We were house-hunting," Douglas informed them.

"House-hunting? What do you mean?" Helen cried.

"Well, it seems that mother feels we need a change —in spite of the fact that she uprooted us from Glen Solan at a moment's notice."

"Yes, go on," Helen prompted, her eyes holding the fear that Arline knew was in her heart. "Where are we going now?"

"Not very far," Douglas replied. "To Winter's Quay, to be exact."

"Because of the yacht racing, I suppose?"

"Well, yes, I expect that was part of the original idea."

"Has mother fixed on a house?" Helen asked.

"Yes, we managed to get nicely settled after a lot of fuss," Douglas admitted.

"Weren't the houses suitable?" Arline asked.

"They looked all right to me," Douglas replied, with all a man's unconcern for domestic detail, "but I soon learned that what was wrong with the first one was all right in the second, but the second was without one of the amenities of the first, and so on. I believe "Thatchwell" was the seventh or eighth we looked over."

"Thatchwell?" Helen repeated. "Has mother actually rented it, then?"

"Yes, I'm afraid so. Don't you feel that a spot of sea air might do you good?"

"I suppose it might," Helen replied slowly, her mind obviously on other things.

"You certainly look as if you need it," Douglas told her with brotherly candour.

"When do we go?" Arline asked.

"Immediately, I think." Douglas turned towards the door. "Anyway, the house is taken now, and there's a regatta next Saturday, so I would say that dad will get us down there as soon as he can."

Arline and Helen followed him into the big square hall. They went up the wide staircase just a little ahead of him.

"I wonder what made mother choose Winter's Quay?" Helen said, when they had gained the first landing. "It's quite near Dunoon, isn't it?"

"Not very far away," Arline replied. "Would you have preferred Dunoon?"

"It doesn't make any difference," Helen said. "I only wondered why she fixed on Winter's Quay. Mother generally has more than one reason for all she does."

"She has this time, too," Douglas informed them airily. "Mother has a great love for some people called McCallum-Blair. And the McCallum-Blairs have a coast house at Winter's Quay."

Arline was not quite sure what she felt in those first moments: she was looking at Helen, and she realised subconsciously that her cousin had turned deathly pale.

Her own white teeth were biting into her lower lip to prevent the exclamation of surprise which almost escaped her at Douglas' announcement, and she followed Helen into her bedroom automatically.

"Well," she said, trying to keep her voice on a light note, "thank goodness we're not going far. It's quite possible to run up to town from Winter's Quay."

Helen raised misty eyes.

"Do you think mother would let us do that?"

"Of course," Arline affirmed, "if we happened to need anything—or you had an appointment at the dressmaker's, say."

Helen gave a little, shaky laugh.

"She'd come with me."

That, Arline thought, was most probable, but it caught at her heart to see Helen's blue eyes so tortured with mingled hope and despair.

"It's not so far from Glasgow to Dunoon," she pointed out, "and even chemists have a half day."

Helen smiled in spite of herself.

"I wish I could be as cheerful as you are over every misfortune, Arline," she said. "You never let things knock you out at one blow as I seem to do. Everything appears black in a moment to me. I've tried to see things differently, but—but I just can't. If only Alex . . ."

"Don't worry," Arline advised. "You'll see him again. We're not going to the coast for good, you know. We'll be back in town for the winter."

"Ah—the winter." Helen's eyes were misty again. "It's not the same, somehow, Arline. I was made for the summer weather, I think—sunshine and blue skies. Alex loves them, too. We often talk of Italy and places where the sun is always shining, and sometimes I long to go right away." She heaved a deep sigh. "But I know that's quite impossible."

"You'll feel all right once you get settled at the coast," Arline said. "It's just that the news has been—rather sudden."

Helen turned from the mirror and swung round on the stool, a faint smile veiling the shadow in her eyes.

"If the McCallum-Blairs have a week-end place at Winter's Quay you might meet Gavin Shandon again," she said.

Arline, whose thoughts had been stirring round this hope ever since Douglas had mentioned the proposed removal, smiled down at her.

"Only if the *Ganta* is there," she said.

"I hope it will be," Helen replied eagerly. "Somehow I think he—you may grow to like him—very much."

The halting statement was half a question, but Arline felt that she could not answer it at that moment, truthfully, even to herself.

As she left Helen and made her way to her own room, she tried to analyse her feelings—tried to do it sanely, deliberately, not allowing her heart to dictate to her too much. She tried to tell herself that she had known Gavin Shandon too short a time to feel anything but a mild interest in him, but somewhere deep within her there was a stirring emotion that she knew she had never experienced before.

With a surge of joy that was almost painful in its intensity, she let the realisation of her love flood over her as she sat in the severe room in the house her aunt had told her would be her home. All bitterness and disappointment seemed to drop from her as she faced the supreme moment in life, and knew that she would no longer journey alone. No word of love had been spoken between them, but in her heart she would carry the emblem of it for all time.

She crossed to the little square of mirror which hung on the wall above her dressing chest. Her face was radiant, her eyes shining with a strange new glow that gave them added depth.

"Gavin," she whispered softly, "Gavin!"

III

The week which followed was a busy one for Arline. Though her aunt frequently took pleasure in telling her acquaintances that Mr. Penner had retired from business, Henry Penner still took quite an active part in the fortunes of Penner's Famous Sauce. He was still the mind behind its continued success, and he was secretly glad that Douglas was eager to go into the business. His son would go in as a director, of course, and not, as Douglas had expressed the wish, to work his way through all the departments so that he might thoroughly understand each working unit.

Arline found herself with more secretarial work than she could cope with comfortably, but she did not complain. The days were winging their way to the week-end, and though she had no reason to hope that Gavin would be at Winter's Quay, her heart sang joyously as she bent to her various tasks, and her fingers flew over the keys of her typewriter with the rapidity of her thoughts.

The domestic staff left for "Thatchwell" immediately after breakfast on the Friday morning, and Mrs. Penner and the two girls took their lunch in an exclusive restaurant in Sauchiehall Street after they had attended to some last minute shopping.

Douglas and the chauffeur set out with the luggage by road, and Arline, sitting in her corner of the first-class carriage with the sun pouring in through the window her aunt had closed, envied them their trip through the glorious countryside.

Mrs. Penner kept to the cabin during the short crossing of the Clyde but Arline and Helen paced the deck, arm in arm, breathing in deep gulps of the invigorating air.

Arline watched the circling sea-gulls and felt that she was on the verge of some strange new experience.

She had been to Winter's Quay before—many times—when her father had taken her on a day's excursion, and they had walked along the shore together talking of all the things they had meant to do in the years ahead of them. She wondered, with a catch at her throat, if Joel Hamilton had known just how short these years were to be.

The steamer was drawing in to Winter's Quay when Mrs. Penner came on deck, and her smile even included Arline as she looked about her, well pleased.

"I hope Alice and Anderson have something ready for us," she said. "The crossing has given me quite an appetite."

The ropes were flung to the quay and fastened securely, the gangway was drawn across the lane of water between steamer and pier, and the purser stood ready to take their tickets. They were the only passengers to disembark, and as they walked down the pier the sounds of the departing boat followed them.

"Oh, look! Dougie's there with the car," Helen cried. "They've been quick, haven't they?"

"I'm glad Douglas had the sense to come and meet us," Mrs. Penner replied, " 'though I hope there has been no dangerous speeding on the way down. Coats is inclined to be a trifle careless, I'm afraid."

Douglas grinned a welcome from the driver's seat of the Daimler, and opened the back door for his mother and Helen, inviting Arline to sit in front with him.

They went slowly along the narrow shore road, and turned up a steep grade where the trees met overhead to form a leafy canopy so thick that there was a perpetual mellow twilight in the little lane. Here and there iron gateways opened in the high beech hedge, and the lane itself ended at two silver painted gates which lay open to admit the car.

The Daimler's wheels crunched over the pebbled drive as it swept up to the main doorway of "Thatchwell."

It was a fine old house, nestling in the arms of the surrounding trees, with a wide, semi-circular sweep of pebbled drive before the two bay windows which flanked the door. Arline, looking down at the unrivalled view across the Firth of Clyde, thought that it must be the finest situated house in Winter's Quay.

Her aunt led them from room to room on a tour of inspection. On the ground floor one room led out of another rather confusingly, and Douglas remarked that the whole place made him think of nothing more than a circular tour. That name was to stick to "Thatchwell" during the time they remained there, and the "circular tour" was to change many things for Arline, things which she could not have imagined on that bright afternoon of her advent at Winter's Quay.

"Arline," Mrs. Penner said after tea, "you know your way about here, I believe?"

"Yes, fairly well," Arline replied.

"Well, I want you to go into Dunoon and open a grocery account right away." She glanced at her watch. "You have even time to go this afternoon. It's not quite five o'clock."

Arline rose from her seat by the window.

"I can get a bus along the shore road," she said, quite glad of the chance to be out in the sunshine. "Can I bring anything back for you?"

"You can call in and get a box of my tablets at the chemist's," her aunt replied. "I must have left my packet at home."

Helen rose from the table, but Mrs. Penner noted the movement and said quickly:

"You'd better come up and help me unpack, Helen."

"I may walk back, Aunt Hilda," Arline suggested. "Supper won't be until ten, I suppose?"

"Yes, ten o'clock," Mrs. Penner replied. "Of course, you'll be home before then."

Making her way back down the shady lane, Arline was just in time to catch a bus which would take her into Dunoon, and, as she rode along with the breeze from the sea coming in at the open window, she gave a deep sigh of contentment.

Dunoon was very busy. It was the height of the holiday season, and the promenade was crowded. The steamers were coming and going at the pier and they were all very full.

Her errand took less than half an hour, and when she came out of the chemist's with her aunt's tablets in her pocket, she wandered idly along the road, gazing in the shop windows as she passed. A small breeze had sprung up, and walking was a delight. When she had left the shops behind, and noted that it was just six o'clock by the post-office clock, she set out for her walk back to Winter's Quay with added enthusiasm.

She swung along easily, choosing the High Road as there was less traffic that way, and humming happily to herself as she went along. Her mood was synonymous with the one of the Sunday morning at Glen Solan when she had run down the grassy slope in the face of the wind.

The thought sent her mind back to Sheena Blair and the little black terrier that had scampered at her heels.

When she saw an identical little terrier trotting round the bend of the road ahead she was tempted to jump to the conclusion that her imagination was playing her tricks. But the dog was real enough. He came scampering up to her, barking noisily.

"Hullo, boy! Where have you come from?" Arline cried.

The little terrier cocked his head at her enquiringly.

He *is* like Sheena McCallum-Blair's Jock, Arline thought, and then decided that all Scotch terriers looked more or less alike. This dog, however, was disposed to be friendly. He turned and followed her back the way he had come, jumping up as far as his stumpy legs would permit, his comical head cocked at an angle each time he stopped to survey her afresh. And Arline, stooping to pat that shaggy head, was unaware, for a moment, that the dog was accompanied. When she straightened at last a man on a bicycle was coming slowly round the bend. When the dog sighted him it ran towards him, barking joyously.

The man had seen her and, dismounting quickly, was at her side.

"Arline!"

"Gavin—!"

They stood looking at one another as if time had been suspended for just that purpose. Arline knew that her pleasure was obvious in her flushed face and sparkling eyes, but she was too happy to care. She had met Gavin Shandon again. She was standing there within a handclasp of him—that was all that seemed to matter for the moment.

"Well, this *is* a surprise." He smiled, and held out his hand. "I had hardly hoped to meet you here."

"Nor I," Arline smiled, warmed by the friendship of his firm handclasp.

"This is where your family moved to, then?" he asked, turning his bicycle round to walk beside her.

"We just arrived to-day," Arline explained. "We went home to Glasgow for a week or two after—after . . ." She stopped, hesitating rather painfully before the memory of that hurried departure from Glen Solan. Then, remembering the cancelled engagement, she continued quickly: "I hope you got my note. It was the only way I had of letting you know that I wouldn't be able to come."

"I got it by the afternoon post—after I had waited for two hours for you," he laughed.

"Oh, I'm so sorry," Arline said. "I should have remembered that there was no Sunday collection."

"Well, suppose we forget about all that now? Now that we've met again. Of course," he added, "I would have found you somewhere—eventually. Are you staying in Dunoon?"

"No. Winter's Quay."

"Better still. Your uncle is down for the regatta?"

"Yes," Arline admitted. "We have taken a house—'Thatchwell.' Do you know it?"

"Very well. We—McCallum-Blair's house is just along the shore."

For some inexplicable reason Arline felt ashamed—ashamed for her aunt and the way Mrs. Penner was virtually shadowing the McCallum-Blairs. In spite of the fact that Gavin was only an employee of the McCallum-Blairs, the feeling was not lessened. She felt that a man of Shandon's type could feel nothing but contempt for Mrs. Penner's tactics.

"Are you racing to-morrow?" she asked, anxious to change the subject.

He shook his head.

"*Ganta* has been playing tricks with us," he laughed. "We had a bit of bad luck at Cowes. She's in for repairs at the Holy Loch and won't take the water again for a week or two."

"How disappointing for you." Arline was genuinely sorry, for she knew how keen Shandon was on the sport. "I've been following all her wins since we left Glen Solan. You did very well in June."

"Not so badly. I'm glad you followed us up—after seeing our first win of the season. I wondered if you would be interested."

He was looking directly down at her, and something very sweet and intimate seemed to vibrate between them. Was it the memory of that swift kiss under the dark trees of Ganavan? She had wanted to be angry with him for that kiss, but she could not be. It had seemed part of the night—inevitable.

"Are you walking home?" Shandon asked, when Jock's impatient barking could no longer be ignored.

"Yes," Arline answered, "I could not resist it on such an evening."

"I'll walk back with you," he said. "Jock has had quite enough exercise for one night." He turned to the dog. "Come on, you restless little devil!"

Jock bounded forward joyfully and was soon lost to sight round the bend of the road.

Shandon and Arline followed more slowly, turning into the side road that would take them down to the shore. As she walked along in the dusky glimmer that the sunshine made as it slanted through the trees, Arline felt a great peace descending upon her. It was a peace of spirit which she had not known for many years—only once, perhaps, since her father's death, and that once on a still evening along the road that led out of Oban to Ganavan. The feeling seemed to be the culminating point of all the happiness she had been so vaguely aware of during the day.

When they reached the narrow path which led round the wall of "Thatchwell" to the green lane, Shandon drew up, leaning against his bicycle.

"I can't promise you a grand-stand view of a good race to-morrow," he said, with one of his slow smiles. "*Ganta* won't be in the race, but I *can* give you a splendid running commentary of events from any given point on the course you care to suggest."

Arline hesitated. She knew that it would be next to impossible to get away from Mrs. Penner's watchful eye, and yet—and yet . . .

"You will come?" There was something forceful in the question. "That last appointment was cancelled against your will, I believe."

"Yes—but I may not be able to get away so—so soon. You see, we've only just arrived."

"To-morrow night, then? Would that be more suitable?" he went on. "You see, I'm determined. I don't mean to go without a promise."

"But," Arline hesitated, "if I fail to keep it again?"

"I'll take it that you did your best to keep it!"

"At six o'clock," Arline called after him, and wondered how she was to escape the Penner vigilance once more.

93

CHAPTER SIX

PUCK WEAVES A SPELL

I

MRS. PENNER was in the best of spirits. It was more than heartening to have received an invitation from Mrs. McCallum-Blair immediately one arrived, she reflected, reading the short, friendly note which had come by the morning post.

Arline knew that the invitation included Mrs. Penner and family, but she was not surprised when her aunt remarked shortly after lunch that she was sure Arline could spend quite an enjoyable evening in the garden, or, failing that, there was always a cinema in Dunoon she might visit.

"I think I can manage to fill the evening in, Aunt Hilda," Arline said lightly.

Things were going even better than she had dared to hope. There would be no questions, no immediate need for explanations which would surely lead to another scene. There was supposed to be a fate that was kind to lovers. Might there not, then, be a fate that was kind to—to people who were happy in each other's company?

Surely—surely nothing could happen to prevent Aunt Hilda from going. Yet, Arline was not wholly at ease until she saw Helen and her mother disappearing down the green lane to where Douglas was waiting with the dinghy to row out to the *Merrimae*.

Though the afternoon stretched blankly before her, it passed at last, and when she had enjoyed a solitary tea in the little morning-room next to the kitchen she went quickly upstairs to her room to change from the print frock she wore to something more suitable to resist the night air.

Her wardrobe was limited, and it did not take her long to choose a neat woollen suit that was both light and warm.

Gavin was already waiting at the foot of the lane when she arrived, though it was still five minutes to six.

"You see, I'm quite punctual this time," Arline laughed. "I only had myself to please all afternoon."

"You mean, you've been alone all the afternoon?" he asked, when he had greeted her.

"Yes, quite alone—enjoying the sunshine."

"What a pity. Had I known, we might have been enjoying it together." He glanced down at his wrist watch. "However, we must make the best of the time we've got. Where would you like to go?"

"You probably know this district much better than I do," Arline suggested. "Can't you think of somewhere?"

"I think I know just the place. Have you ever been to Puck's Glen?" he asked.

"No. What is it like? It sounds rather worth-while with a name like that," Arline replied.

"It's the sort of place you'd love," he told her gravely, "and it's not too far away."

"Shall we go, then?" she asked, eager to make a start.

"I'm afraid it will have to be by bus this time," he said, as they set off along the coast road.

"I love riding in these quaint little buses," Arline replied promptly.

"Then we're in luck," he smiled. "There's one coming right behind us."

When they were comfortably seated, he proceeded to point out the various landmarks to her as they went along. At the head of the Holy Loch he indicated the slipway where the *Ganta* was undergoing repairs, and they even caught a glimpse of her familiar scarlet and white lines as they passed the open door of the yard.

"You'll be glad when she's back in the water again," Arline said, as they drew away from the straggling line of houses along the road that wound into the hills.

He smiled gravely.

"I'm afraid my racing days are over for this season," he said. "I have other work to attend to which, in spite of my love of racing, is more important at the moment."

He would be going away! The thought struck Arline with the force of a blow. She had imagined that now they had met they need not part again so swiftly.

The bus was going slowly across a narrow bridge beneath which a brown river gurgled and laughed between the grey stones, and soon they drew up before the rustic archway which led into Puck's Glen. As they climbed up into the arboretum Shandon became noticeably silent. His face was grave, but the stern look she remembered so well from their first encounter was gone. He had the look of a man who was weighing a decision for the final time.

Arline looked about her. It was cool and quiet here among the giant trees with the sunlight slanting through like golden gauze spread across the lichen-covered paths. When they reached the top of the hill, at last, she sank down on one of the rustic seats which overlooked the gorge and heaved a deep sigh of contentment.

"It's heavenly," she breathed. "Heavenly!"

"I knew you would like it," he said, coming over to sit by her side. "Was it worth the climb?"

"More than worth it," she declared, her eyes shining.

She did not want to talk, somehow. It was enough to sit here far up on the hillside among the trees with Gavin by her side and all the world so far away that it scarcely seemed to exist at all. Only the blue cloud-flecked sky above them and the glimpse of green hills between the trees was reality. Everything she had left behind at "Thatchwell" was a dream—a troubled dream from which she had just awakened to the security of the present. Out here everything was fresh and unsullied: the wind that strayed among the trees was a gentle wind; the tops of the silver firs stirred softly to its caress, and the green rain of the larch hung down above the murmuring water in the gorge below.

"I've never seen so many glorious trees," Arline said at last, her eyes roving the length of the glen and back again to the gorge at their feet.

"Not even at Ganavan?"

His voice held a deep, vibrating note which stirred a chord in her own heart. She turned slowly and looked at him.

"Arline, I had meant to speak to you about Ganavan if we had met that morning at Glen Solan," he began, "but the interval of our parting has made no difference to what I want to say to you."

"Yes?"

Arline's reply was barely audible, and it seemed to sink

away to the very heart of Puck's wood before he spoke again.

"Arline, haven't you guessed it, my dear? I love you." His lips were very close to her hair, and she could feel his quickened breathing as he waited. "Dearest—what have you to say to me?"

She could not say anything at first. The moment was hers out of a world which had not proved too kind to her in the past, and she clung to it jealously lest she should awake to find it gone from her for ever.

"Arline!" Gently but firmly he turned her round to face him, and his grey eyes looked down into her own misted dark ones.

"Gavin!"

She put out her hand to him, and instantly it was imprisoned in his while his other arm went round her shoulders, drawing her closer. But he did not attempt to kiss her again until, at last, she lifted her head of her own accord and shyly offered him her lips.

Time seemed to slip away from them; they were caught up in a spell which can only be experienced once in a lifetime—the spell of love which, if not brought to fulfilment, will haunt the lonely heart for ever afterwards.

The sky had turned pale gold above the shoulders of the western hills before they moved, and Arline lifted her head from his arm where she had pillowed it confidently. Their eyes met, and again he drew her to him for one long, deep kiss.

"Arline, beloved, how beautiful you are," he whispered, as he rose and helped her to her feet. "I never dreamed that life could be like this."

She put her arms round his neck and kissed him impulsively.

"Life has changed for me, too, since this afternoon," she said with a shy smile. "You have changed it all. Oh, Gavin, I'm so happy. I'm so happy I want to cry!"

"Don't, my darling! Your eyes were made for laughter, not for tears."

His face was grave again as he released her, and she saw the frown that marked two pencil lines between his brows. What had displeased him, she wondered, but knew, instinctively, that his displeasure was not with her.

1095

When they were going down through the gorge where the water tumbled over the stones, he took her hand and drew it through his arm.

"Arline, I don't want us to wait very long," he said. "I want you to marry me right away after the shortest possible engagement. Will you?"

He paused, bending to look into her eyes. What he saw there made Arline's wavering "yes" quite unnecessary.

They caught the last bus from the glen with a fraction of a second to spare. It was crowded with picnickers from Benmore, and they were forced to sit apart, but each shy glance she directed at his broad back in the seat in front of her renewed the joy of that confession on the hillside for Arline.

They walked slowly up the green lane together, hand in hand, like two happy children, pausing just outside the silver gates of "Thatchwell."

"I'll come round and speak to your uncle about our plans when we have had time to make them," Gavin said, "or would you prefer me to see him right away?"

For the first time Arline remembered the Penners, and the memory of many scenes in her domestic surroundings brought the first cloud to her shining horizon.

"No," she said hurriedly, "I'd better tell them myself."

"Arline, there's something else I want to say—something I should have told you long ago, I'm afraid."

He paused, and in that instant the voice of Mrs. Penner came up through the silence of the green lane to where they stood:

"I suppose Arline will be home by this time—indeed, I expect it."

Arline turned swiftly to her companion.

"It's my aunt and the family," she whispered. "Gavin, I must go—really, I must, before they come."

She did not want a scene: she did not want one breath of discord to spoil the most glorious day of her life.

He caught her to him in the dusk and pressed his lips to hers.

"To-morrow," he said, "I want you to come and meet my mother."

"I'll be at the end of the lane," Arline breathed.

"Six o'clock, then! Good night, my beloved."

Arline was gone before the Penners reached the bend of the lane.

Shandon passed them on his way down. They were discussing the evening spent in the company of the McCallum-Blairs.

II

"Aunt Hilda, I'm going out after tea, if you don't mind," Arline said, shutting and opening the book she had been reading all afternoon.

In spite of her resolution of the morning, she was nervous —horribly nervous of another scene, she acknowledged, as she noticed her aunt's upraised eyebrows and met the cold blue eyes beneath them.

"And may I ask where?"

"I—I've met someone I care for and—and we want to become engaged soon. Gavin wants me to meet his mother to-night."

Her halting little confession ended lamely before her aunt's concentrated stare.

"Indeed!"

It was the only word Mrs. Penner seemed capable of for the moment.

"Yes," Arline rushed on, not waiting to choose her words, "I meant to tell you this morning—earlier—but there hasn't been an opportunity."

"Perhaps you mean that you had no intention of telling me anything about your plans for your future had you been able to slip away undetected." Mrs. Penner had recovered from her first surprise, and she was herself again.

"Oh, yes, I would have told you—indeed I would," Arline said quickly.

"Well, who is this man?" her aunt demanded.

For the fraction of a second Arline hesitated. The time had come to tell the truth, and she knew there would be a scene, but she was determined to stand her ground. Nothing Mrs. Penner could say or do could shake her determination this time. They had all given in too often.

"Gavin is the man who came to my assistance at Glen Solan when I upset the boat," she explained.

It seemed to Arline that they sat there facing each other for an eternity before her aunt's wrath formed itself in words.

"That man!" Mrs. Penner cried, jumping to her feet. "Have you taken complete leave of your senses? Are you trying to tell me that you are thinking of becoming engaged to him?"

"Yes," Arline returned calmly. "I am thinking of —just that. Perhaps when you meet him you will understand . . ."

"Meet him? You're not suggesting that I should receive him here, are you?" Mrs. Penner was aghast.

"I thought you might. Gavin expects to—to see Uncle Henry before we become engaged."

Mrs. Penner gave an unpleasant little laugh.

"You have kept this thing so much of a secret up to now, Arline, that you can hardly expect us to rush and receive your—young man"—she used the words deliberately, in the tone she reserved for the affairs of her servants —"with open arms at a moment's notice."

Arline flushed, but she ignored the slight in the words.

"I'm sorry that you feel that way about it, Aunt Hilda," she said, striving to remain calm.

"Is there any other way I might feel about such an affair?" Mrs. Penner demanded. "You knew of my displeasure over the incident right from the beginning, and yet you go on to cultivate this man's acquaintance and finally propose to become engegaed to him—to a common deck hand. May I enquire how you intend to live— and on what?"

Arline was more angry than she had ever been in her life, but she struggled to regain her composure.

"Gavin isn't on the yacht all the time," she said, "he —he has some other work in—in Glasgow, I think."

She realised, suddenly, just how little she knew of his life apart from his interest in yachting, but that had not seemed to matter until now. Mrs. Penner, however, was only too eager to pounce upon this fact to her niece's disadvantage.

"As I thought," she remarked acidly, "you scarcely know a thing about the man. I would have thought that a girl of your age would have had more sense than to allow herself to be infatuated to this extent."

"I don't think it's infatuation, Aunt Hilda," Arline replied quietly. "I prefer to call it love."

"Call it what you like," Mrs. Penner rejoined. "I call it nonsense—stupidity, gross stupidity. You can't seriously hope to live decently on anything a man in his unsettled position can provide, and if he is hoping that you will be able to take advantage of your uncle's position to sponge on him . . ."

"Aunt Hilda—please stop!" Arline was very pale, and her hands were clenched at her side. "We won't sponge —or ask for anything. Gavin would be the last person on earth to do such a thing. He's much too proud."

"Proud of what?" Mrs. Penner asked dryly.

"There is a pride quite apart from the pride of possession."

Arline could not help the snub. It was hard to remain calm before her aunt's insults, but she knew that there was still something else to tell Mrs. Penner. The fact that Gavin had been working on the McCallum-Blairs' yacht could no longer be kept a secret, and she preferred that the information should come from herself rather than as gossip between Mrs. McCallum-Blair and her aunt.

"There's something else I think you should know." she went on. "Gavin was employed on Mr. McCallum-Blair's yacht at Glen Solan."

Mrs. Penner sank down on a nearby chair and passed her hand over her eyes.

"No, it can't be true! I can't be asked to believe such a thing," she cried.

Arline stood where she was in the centre of the room, waiting.

At last Mrs. Penner rose, and the fury in her blue eyes was almost fanatical.

"How could you? What have I ever done to you to deserve this? One insult after another. It is unthinkable that anyone could be so ungrateful. You know how much I am depending on the McCallum-Blairs' friendship for Helen's sake, and you stand there quite calmly and tell me you propose to become engaged to one of their hired servants. I tell you I forbid it—absolutely forbid it!"

Arline sighed wearily. It was being harder than she had expected.

"I'm sorry to seem ungrateful, Aunt Hilda," she said, "but I don't think my being engaged to Gavin should make any difference to your friendship with Mrs. McCallum-Blair."

"You don't? Well, I should hardly have expected you to see my point of view, of course. It is just another example of your complete selfishness, Arline. I suppose the fact that I am expecting Mrs. McCallum-Blair to pay me a social visit to-morrow afternoon for the first time will make very little difference to you."

"If there's anything I could do about it . . ." Arline hesitated.

"There is. Keep this unfortunate engagement of yours out of the limelight for a day or two, at least. I suppose I have no right to expect anything more." Mrs. Penner gave a sigh and turned to the door.

"Gavin is leaving Winter's Quay, Aunt Hilda," Arline said quickly. "After all, Mrs. McCallum-Blair may not be interested in his affairs after he has gone."

"I hope not. Anyway, there is no need to blazon the fact that you have become engaged to an ex-deck hand all over Winter's Quay. At least, you can concede that much to my feelings."

With this parting shot she swept from the room, leaving Arline to gaze rather wistfully out of the window.

She knew that she could not give Gavin Shandon up, but she would try to meet her aunt half way and ask him to agree to a secret engagement for a month or two.

As she went outside into the garden, however, she became increasingly sure that Gavin would frown on such a proposal. She could picture the flash of disdain in his grey eyes as she suggested it. No, he would want to proclaim their engagement to the world. He would be proud of it—as she was proud of it—and she could not see him allowing Mrs. Penner to interfere.

III

Arline had slept little the night before, and, though her thoughts were far from peaceful, the lazy quiet of the

Sunday afternoon lulled her into a semi-drowsiness. She was screened from sight of the drive by the trees, and there was only the open stretch of the Firth before her.

It was someone shaking her gently that brought her back to complete consciousness. Helen was bending over her chair, her face flushed, her eyes shining.

"Arline! Arline, wake up!"

"Hullo Helen! I wasn't really asleep," Arline protested, but her cousin laughed gaily.

"Now, don't prevaricate," she said. "You know you were, but I really don't blame you. It's so very warm."

"Is all that flushed look of yours entirely due to the weather?" Arline asked with a smile, sitting up to survey her cousin.

Helen glanced quickly towards the house.

"Arline," she whispered. "I've seen Alex."

"Where? When?"

"Here—this afternoon. He's been down for the day," Helen continued quickly. "He told me he would come before we left Glasgow, and—forgive me, dear—I heard mother arguing with you after lunch and I was heartless enough to seize my opportunity."

"That wasn't heartless," Arline laughed, "it was sensible. But how did Alex know where to meet you?"

"We had arranged that he should be on the back road during the afternoon, and if there was the slightest chance at all, I would slip away."

"I see," Arline replied. "So you met him without any trouble?"

"Yes. We went round by Loch Losken." She smiled reminiscently, and Arline gave her hand a friendly squeeze.

"Well, they say it's an ill wind that blows nobody good," she said lightly. "I'm glad something pleasant transpired during my unpleasant half hour."

"Oh, Arline, you must think I'm a beast taking advantage of mother rowing you like that. I really felt mean, you know."

Arline shrugged.

"You couldn't have helped by staying behind. In fact, you were better with Alex," she said.

"What was the row about this time?" Helen asked, her eyes troubled.

Arline would have liked to have confided in Helen completely, but she had promised Mrs. Penner to say nothing of the engagement, and her inherent sense of loyalty once a promise had been given bade her keep the information even from her cousin.

"Oh," she replied, "more or less the same old subject. I told Aunt Hilda about Gavin, and I'm afraid the news upset her a little."

"You mean, you told her about—about the McCallum-Blairs? About Gavin being on their yacht?"

Arline nodded.

"Oh, Arline. Were you not terribly afraid?"

"I wasn't *afraid*, Helen," Arline replied, "but it was all rather unpleasant. I see your mother's point, of course, about the McCallum-Blairs. If Mrs. McCallum-Blair is inclined to be a snob, it must be—unfortunate for Aunt Hilda that things have turned out this way."

"Why did you tell her?" Helen asked.

"Because I met Gavin again yesterday."

"Oh, how splendid! I knew you would," Helen cried. "Where?"

"On my way back from Dunoon," Arline replied. "I've had no opportunity to tell you. I went to meet him again last night."

It was hard not to confide in Helen, she thought, as she saw the light of interest deepening in her cousin's blue eyes.

"Are you going to meet him again?" Helen asked.

"Yes—to-night," Arline smiled. "Which reminds me, I want to change before tea. Do you?"

"Yes, I think I had better," Helen said, glancing down at her dusty shoes. "I don't feel quite able to thinking up an alibi for my travel-stained appearance."

They went into the house together and met Alice in the hall.

"Where's mother?" Helen asked the girl. "Is she still resting?"

"Oh, no, miss," Alice replied. "She got up quite a while back an' she's in the drawing-room with a visitor. She sent word that you were to go in immediately you got back, Miss Helen."

"I can't go in like this," Helen said. "I must slip upstairs and change first. Who's the visitor, Alice? Do you know?"

"The gentleman said he was Mrs. McCallum-Blair's son, miss," Alice replied, and Arline saw every vestige of colour draining out of Helen's face.

When they reached her bedroom Helen sank down on the bed.

"Did you hear what she said?" she asked numbly.

Arline sat down beside her.

"Don't let things upset you so, Helen," she urged. "What harm is there in a call from Mrs. McCallum-Blair's son?"

"I tell you I don't want to meet him," Helen cried. "I won't be forced into being pleasant to him just because he *is* somebody and has lots of money and a good social position."

"I'm not suggesting that you should be unduly nice to him," Arline said patiently, "but there can be no harm in meeting him. No one can *force* you to marry him, Helen. The days for that sort of thing are long since past."

"You don't know mother very well," Helen declared. "Once she makes up her mind, she has her way no matter how many hearts she tramples on to achieve that end."

Arline knew that Helen was seeing things through the hazy glass of desperation. Yet she could not urge her cousin to take a firm stand about Alex for the simple reason that she knew that Helen was not strong enough to follow up the first attack. Mrs. Penner would win in the end, a forceful, dominating victory that would crush the frail soul of her daughter completely.

"I know you think I should stand up to things," Helen said unsteadily, "but I can't. Sometimes the urge to tell mother the truth almost overcomes my fear of her, but then I begin to think—to think of every incident in the past when I ever dared to thwart her or question her authority. I wish I felt strong enough—for Alex's sake."

"Has Alex ever spoken of—seeing your mother and father?" Arline asked.

"Yes—once or twice, but I've always put him off— asked him to wait and leave it to me, and I know—I *know* I'll never be able to do anything about it."

It was only too obvious that Helen was passing as much time as possible upstairs before she went down to the drawing-room to meet her mother's unexpected guest, but at last she let the heavy enamel-backed comb clatter on the crystal tray and turned slowly from the dressing-table.

"Do you think I might plead a headache?" she asked. "Arline, you could go and tell mother I was lying down, couldn't you?"

The eagerness in eyes and voice was pitiful. Arline went swiftly across the room and put both hands on Helen's shoulders.

"I would," she said, "willingly—if it was going to do the slightest bit of good. Don't you see, Helen, the longer you shirk a thing the more formidable it becomes to your mind. It's like—going to the destist's. Go down and get it over. You'll have to meet him some time, won't you?"

"Yes, I suppose so."

"Then, why not now? You may only have to engage him in polite conversation for a very short time."

"Mother is sure to invite him to tea," Helen surmised.

"Well, even if she does, the man can't pick you up and run away with you!"

"All the same," Helen sighed, "I wish he hadn't come."

Arline gave her a gentle shake, though there was no trace of impatience in her voice as she said lightly:

"Has it never occurred to you that this young man is probably quite capable of taking an instant dislike to you?"

"Oh—do you think he might?"

"He may have a definite antipathy to blondes with large blue eyes," Arline pointed out.

"I never thought of that," Helen said naively.

"Didn't you think it possible?" Arline teased, glad that the conversation had developed a lighter side.

"You know I hate conceited people," Helen replied. "I wonder what *he's* like? Probably he's self-opinionated and terribly sure of himself."

"Are you being fair?" Arline asked, on her way to the door. "He may be shy and self-conscious and dreadfully nervous."

"I wonder which would be worse." Helen was able to laugh a little now. "Though I still think he'll come under the first category."

"Well, hadn't you better go and see?" Arline suggested. "Aunt Hilda will be expecting you."

The smile left Helen's face as quickly as it had come.

"But aren't you coming down with me, Arline?" she asked. "I need your support, you know."

Arline was quite sure that Mrs. Penner would want Helen's presence downstairs alone for the short time which still remained before tea, and she was not anxious to court her aunt's displeasure anew by presenting herself to make an unwanted fourth in the drawing-room.

"I'll come down presently," she promised. "I can't appear in this state when there's company."

"You won't be too long—promise," Helen begged. "Douglas is out, and there will be just mother and me downstairs."

"All right, I promise," Arline smiled. "Give me five minutes to change, and I'll come down and support you all I can."

IV

Arline's eyes were shining as she selected a simple afternoon dress from her wardrobe and slipped it over her head. She drew the comb through her thick hair and pressed the waves into some semblance of order, conjecturing up an image of Gavin's mother in her mind. She pictured her a dear old lady with a kindly smile and grey, far-seeing eyes like those of her son. Her heart began to beat faster as she realised that in little more than an hour she was about to have the first glimpse into the family life of the man who had come to mean so much to her in so short a time.

What had Gavin told his mother about her?

She leaned nearer to the mirror and smiled a little at her reflection.

"To-night I am going to meet her," she said aloud.

She went slowly along the corridor. She supposed it was quite all right to put in an appearance now, and she had promised Helen that she would not stay away too long.

When she came within sight of the hall she noticed that the drawing-room door was open.

"It's very good of you to ask me, Mrs. Penner, but I'm afraid I must refuse this time. My mother will be expecting

107

me for tea, and I have an appointment immediately afterwards."

The words floated up to the watcher on the stairs, but their meaning was completely lost to her. One fact, and one alone, stood out for Arline. She knew that voice. It had become familiar—so dearly familiar—during the past few weeks, and her trembling limbs almost refused to support her as her lips framed one name.

"Gavin. Gavin Shandon!"

Arline was powerless to move. She stood there as if she had been turned to stone and saw Gavin's tall figure framed in the drawing-room doorway and watched him coming down the long, narrow hall. Words were running round in her mind in hopeless confusion. Mrs. McCallum-Blair's son . . . the gentleman said he was Mrs. McCallum-Blair's son . . . you are to go to the drawing-room immediately, Miss Helen . . . the gentleman said he was Mrs. McCallum-Blair's son . . .

Suddenly Gavin looked up and saw her standing there. Without a moment's hesitation he was by her side.

The look in Arline's eyes must have given him som indication that she had guessed the truth, for he made n attempt at preliminary greetings. He took her hand firml between his own and said quietly:

"I'm not going to attempt to explain anything here Arline. Are you still willing to meet me to-night?"

Arline looked down at him and found herself nodding dumbly.

"My mother has been taken ill rather suddenly," he went on, "so I'm afraid I can't ask you to come to Rowan Gate to meet her to-night." He glanced at his watch. "Will you be at the end of the lane at seven o'clock?"

"Yes."

Her reply was little more than a whisper. He gave her hand a reassuring clasp, and she watched him go as if from some great distance. Then she drew in a deep breath and walked towards the drawing-room door.

Mrs. Penner was sitting on the settee at the window, a smile of satisfaction on her lips, but one glance at Helen told Arline that her cousin had stumbled on the identity of Mrs. McCallum-Blair's son. Helen's face was flushed and her eyes were unnaturally bright. She seemed hardly able to control her desire to speak to Arline.

"Mrs. McCallum-Blair's son has just called," Mrs. Penner informed Arline conversationally, as Alice entered with the tea-tray. "Such a charming young man!"

Her aunt's voice seemed to be floating somewhere far above her head as Arline accepted her tea-cup and made an effort to eat two fingers of toast. Her mind, crowded with a thousand questions, could find an answer to none of them. All she seemed aware of was that Gavin Shandon was not what he had represented himself to be.

In that first moment of confusion it did not occur to her that it had been her own conjecture that had placed Shandon as the deck-hand on the McCallum-Blair's yacht, and his only fault had been in not correcting her.

Now that she knew the truth, what was she going to do?

Before the solution of that problem could shape itself in her mind other thoughts were crowding it out. What would Mrs. Penner say when she found out—as she inevitably would find out? The McCallum-Blairs? Helen? Everybody. Why had things to happen like this? Why had Gavin let her believe something that was not true?

"I must drop a note to Mrs. McCallum-Blair," Mrs. Penner said, rising at last. "I'm so sorry she is ill. Arline, you can put it in the pillar-box for me when you go out."

As soon as her mother had left the room Helen jumped up and crossed to Arline's side.

"Arline—did you know all the time?" she asked breathlessly.

Arline shook her head.

"You don't think I would have played that sort of trick," she said rather abruptly.

Helen sat down on the arm of her cousin's chair.

"No," she said, "I don't think you would. I shouldn't have asked you that. What I meant was—had you no idea that Gavin was—well, not ordinary?"

"I hadn't thought of anything like that," Arline replied. "I suppose I was only too ready to take him at face value."

"But you're surely not *angry* at how things have turned out?" Helen asked quickly.

"No, I'm not angry—just perhaps a little bit disappointed."

"Disappointed? But, how can you be? He's—it's much better than it might have been, isn't it? I mean, you won't have to worry about saving up to get married or anything now," Helen pointed out.

"No, I suppose not—if you look at it that way," Arline said, "but I was quite willing to worry about saving up to be married when I thought he was comparatively poor. . . ."

Her eyes were misty. She felt that she had lost something that she had prized, yet she could not put a name to it. Perhaps it was trust.

"I thought I could have trusted him to the end of the earth," she said, hardly conscious that she had uttered the thought aloud.

"Did he actually *tell* you that he worked for the McCallum-Blairs?" Helen asked.

"No," Arline said slowly, "I suppose he didn't — actually. . . ."

"Then, is it really fair to blame him?" Helen asked. "As far as I can see, what he did was very human. You jumped to a wrong conclusion and, as he found himself beginning to care for you, he preferred to win you as the poor yacht hand rather than as McCallum-Blair's son."

Was there something in what Helen said? Arline's heart leapt at the joy of it.

"Do you think so?" she said a little nervously.

"Of course. What other reason could there be?" Helen cried, glad that her attempt to bring Arline out of her despairing mood had succeeded a little.

"But—to give me a wrong name—to call himself Gavin Shandon," Arline half objected.

"That *is* his name," Helen said. "He explained to mother. You see, Mrs. McCallum-Blair has been married twice, and Gavin is the son of her first marriage. Mr. McCallum-Blair is his step-father."

Helen was clearing up point after point with happy confidence, and Arline suddenly thought of all Mrs. Penner had planned for her daughter. This last turn of events had complicated things more than ever. What would her aunt say when she discovered the truth? It did not bear thinking about.

"You're going to meet him, aren't you?" Helen asked. "You can't mean to give him up just because of this?"

There was urgency in the question, and Arline tried to smile.

"Yes, I'll go to meet him," she said, as the door opened and Mrs. Penner re-entered the room, the letter to Mrs. McCallum-Blair in her hand.

Arline rose and took it automatically.

"You wont' forget to post it?" Mrs. Penner said, "and please remember to get back home at a reasonable hour."

Arline had left her scarf on the chest in the hall, and she caught it up now and made her way slowly down the drive. For the first time since that swift revelation of Gavin's identity she was alone, but her thoughts still persisted in circling round the trivial aspects of the situation, refusing to concentrate on any of the main issues. She wondered, over and over again, what Shandon would have to say to her—what explanation he would offer—and then some little irrelevant incident in the past would rise and blot out all other thoughts. It was useless to reason round and round in these interminable circles, she told herself, at last, as she reached the end of the green lane and looked about her.

Though it was after seven o'clock, the lane and the long stretch of coast road lay deserted before her. Gavin Shandon had not put in an appearance. For another five minutes she waited, watching idly and hardly conscious of what she saw.

Ten minutes went past, and she decided to walk to the corner of the road and post Mrs. Penner's letter. Queer to be posting a letter from Aunt Hilda to Gavin's mother!

Dropping the letter into the post-box, she turned to retrace her steps to the corner of the lane. She passed it and walked on, slowly at first, and then her steps began to quicken in time to her racing thoughts. She was almost at the Point when a car swung out between the gateposts of a house which was hidden behind a thick row of mountain ash. She recognised it immediately; it was the sports car which had carried Gavin and her to Oban that day—so long ago now, it seemed.

The car drew up on the other side of the road, and Shandon leaned over the steering-wheel. His face was strangely pale under his coating of tan, and his eyes were troubled.

111

"Arline." He opened the door and motioned to her to get in. "I'm sorry I've had to keep you waiting, but I couldn't get here any quicker."

His voice was gruff, almost curt, and he closed the door as soon as she had sunk into the seat beside him.

"That's all right," she said, feeling that some remark was necessary. "There has been no—trouble, I hope?"

"I'm afraid there has." He started the car again and drove swiftly along the coast road. "I haven't got a great deal of time for explanations now. I must get to Dunoon and back as quickly as I can—it's urgent. My mother has been taken rather seriously ill while I was out this afternoon, and the doctor fears that an operation may be necessary."

"Oh, I'm sorry." Arline was immediately concerned for him. "Gavin," she said, after a moment's consideration, "don't worry about me. I must only be in the way just now. Put me down here and I can walk back."

There was a measure of relief in his grey eyes as he slowed the car.

"It's good of you to understand," he said. "After I go to Dunoon I must go straight to Glasgow. This doctor wants other advice."

Arline got out of the car and stood with her hands resting on the top of the door.

"I hope your mother will be all right," she said huskily. She was not thinking of the invalid as Mrs. McCallum-Blair, but as Gavin's mother. He bent forward and put his hand over hers.

"Arline—about this afternoon. So many explanations are necessary. I tried to tell you last night at the gate before your people came. I had no right to let you believe what I did, but I had a reason for it—a reason I haven't time to explain now. The whole affair has been a complete mix-up from beginning to end. I should never have entered into it in the first place and avoided all this muddle."

His lips were a firm line, and the worried expression in his eyes deepened. Arline felt a rush of tenderness surging through her, and her fingers closed over his hand.

"Don't worry about it," she urged. "I—I think I understand without explanations."

112

He looked at her for a moment, doubtfully, and then he smiled faintly.

"Thank you, Arline," he said at last. "Your understanding is a help."

"Please go on now," she said. "I don't want to keep you another minute."

He let in his clutch.

"I'll write—just as soon as I can," he promised, and the car slipped noiselessly away along the winding road.

CHAPTER SEVEN

FLIGHT

I

TWO days after Gavin Shandon's departure for Glasgow a package and a letter were delivered at "Thatchwell" addressed to Arline. Mrs. Penner eyed both suspiciously as she handed them over to her niece.

"Something for you, Arline," she said, and her tone implied that she was waiting for Arline to open them in her presence.

Arline slit the envelope and extracted the thick sheet of notepaper. It bore the address and telephone number of a Glasgow club, and, as her eyes caught the hastily-scrawled signature at the end of the brief epistle, her heart began to pound.

"Dear Arline," she read,

"I am sending you a ring—our engagement ring—which I hope you will like and trust will fit you, as I had to guess the size.

"My mother is a little better, and there may not be any necessity to operate after all. This, as you will guess, is a great relief to me. Meanwhile, I am being kept very busy in town, but I hope to get down to Winter's Quay by the week-end.

"Yours, in great haste,
"Gavin."

In spite of herself a little chill went through Arline. The letter was so unlike Gavin—the Gavin she had known and come to love. And then she gave herself a little mental shake and told herself that anyone half crazy with anxiety at their mother's illness and snowed under with work as he confessed himself to be could scarcely be expected to pen an elaborate love letter. It had been more than thoughtful of him to spare the time to choose a ring in the midst of all his worry.

Fully conscious of Mrs. Penner's scrutiny, but determined that she was not going to open her precious parcel under her aunt's hostile gaze, she lifted the small package and carried it up to her room. There, with the door closed firmly against intruders, she broke the seal.

The paper fell apart to disclose a square, velvet box. Arline's fingers were trembling as she pressed the catch, and the lid sprang back to reveal three flawless diamonds in a cross-way setting, sparkling against the velvet cushion of the box. She gave a tiny gasp of mingled astonishment and joy as she looked down at the beautiful ring.

"Oh, Gavin," she whispered, "it's lovely—lovely!"

She lifted it out, slowly and carefully, as if the very beauty of it must make it frail, and slipped it on to the third finger of her left hand. Somehow she felt that Gavin should have done that, but it could not be helped. The ring fitted perfectly.

Then and there she sat down at the small table near the window and penned the contents of her full heart to the man she loved.

Addressing it to the club, she carried her letter downstairs and placed it with the pile of outgoing mail on the hall table.

Helen was somewhere in the garden. Arline had seen her wandering idly among the rhododendron bushes from the bedroom window, and she felt that she must share her news with her cousin. She was human enough to want Helen to praise her ring.

Quite naturally she shrank from imparting the news to Mrs. Penner. She thought, with a wry smile, that her interviews with her aunt were slowly developing into a series of unpleasant scenes. And Mrs. Penner had still to learn Gavin's real identity.

She searched the full length of the garden, but could not find any trace of Helen, and concluded that Douglas must have persuaded her to join him on one of his numerous fishing excursions to the Holy Loch. She made her way back to the house rather slowly. Entering by the morning-room window, which opened directly on to the side of the drive and was used as frequently as the door, she passed on through the dining-room to the hall beyond. After the bright sunshine outside the gloom within made everything rather indistinct, but as her eyes became accustomed to the subdued light she became aware of Mrs. Penner standing by the hall table with a letter in her hand.

It took Arline several seconds to realise that it was her reply to Gavin which her aunt was holding out towards her.

"What is the meaning of this?" Mrs. Penner asked, at last.

"I beg your pardon?"

Arline could not keep the icy note from her voice, and she was conscious that her hands were trembling with the desire to snatch her letter from the woman who stood in her path.

"I am demanding an explanation," Mrs. Penner said, and, holding up the envelope, read aloud: "Mr. Gavin Shandon. What right have you to communicate with Mrs. McCallum-Blair's son?"

Something seemed to snap in Arline's brain. She had an almost overwhelming desire to laugh, and then to cry. These scenes were becoming far too frequent, and her nerves were rebelling against the strain. She could not continue in her endeavour to keep the peace against such odds.

"Every right in the world," she cried at last. "I am replying to a letter and the gift of a ring from my fiancé— the man I am going to marry."

Mrs. Penner could not mistake the meaning of those words, nor did she pretend to. The only sign she gave that she had been dealt a staggering blow was to grip the edge of the heavily-carved table.

"So, this is how you repay our kindness to you?" Her voice was so low as to be a little more than a whisper— a sound like the hiss of a snake. "You've been laughing at us, I expect, laughing behind our backs while you told the story of your deck-hand and the man who saved your life."

"Gavin *is* the man who saved my life at Glen Solan, Aunt Hilda. Please take my word for it—I didn't know he was Mrs. McCallum-Blair's son until—until long afterwards."

"Take your word for it!" Mrs. Penner gave a harsh laugh. "Do you seriously think I can take your word for anything now? We have done everything for you—given you a home, clothes, your keep, the benefit of our surroundings—and what have you done in return?"

A vision of the accumulated secretarial work of years rose before Arline, but she bit her lip and refrained from making any reply.

"This is the way you think fit to repay us," Mrs. Penner went on. "To creep behind our backs and spoil Helen's chances."

"Aunt Hilda—I assure you I had no idea who Gavin was until——"

"Well, when did you discover that your penniless deckhand was a wealthy stockbroker and the son of one of my valued friends?" Mrs. Penner demanded.

"Only—on Sunday."

Arline had not meant to admit that Gavin had kept the truth of his identity from her for so long, and something about the look which passed over Mrs. Penner's face made her wish that she had kept her own counsel. It was too late now, however, and there was also a feeling of relief that the whole truth had been told at last.

"I see." Mrs. Penner's mouth was a thin scarlet line as she eyed her niece. "Well," she continued, throwing the letter back on the pile on the post tray, "I suppose I should be ready for anything now, and never be surprised again."

It was fully a minute before Arline moved. Automatically she crossed to the table, lifted her letter, and went out to post it herself. As she walked down the green lane her aunt's words seemed to sound after her, hounding her on, faster and faster, until she was almost running when she reached the road.

II

It seemed to Arline that her aunt's attitude was strangely passive during the next two days. Mrs. Penner made no further reference to her niece's engagement.

Douglas had been frank and sincere in his congratulations.

"I always knew he was the right sort, Arline," he had said, "a McCallum-Blair or no McCallum-Blair," and Arline had laughed at the blunt compliment, while she had thanked him inwardly for it.

A note came for Mrs. Penner by the morning post on Friday and, when she had read it, she placed it carefully in the pocket of her house coat and smiled across at the other members of the family who were gathered round the breakfast table.

"Just a short note from Mrs. McCallum-Blair," she explained." She is a little better now, and says she would be glad to have me call in the near future." She rose from the table and crossed to the door. "I think I will run along for a few minutes after lunch," she continued. "Even though I don't see her, I can always enquire how she is."

"Hadn't you better wait a day or two if she's been all that ill?" Douglas asked bluntly.

"I don't think so, Douglas," his mother replied. "Mrs. McCallum-Blair expressed a definite wish to see me."

Arline looked up. Had there been a faint stress on those last few words? If so, Mrs. Penner's expression gave no intimation that it had been intentional. Arline dismissed the impression from her mind, fearing that she was becoming over-sensitive, and accepted Douglas' invitation to spear flounders at the head of the loch.

There was an art in spearing flounders. Arline discovered this fact after an hour in which she lay over the side of the small boat and speared anything and everything but a flounder.

They rowed back leisurely, taking an oar apiece, and matching stroke for stroke. Arline, with the knowledge in her heart that she was about to give up all these pleasant hours with her cousin, felt a strange lump rise in her throat.

Douglas beached the boat.

"Perhaps you'd better go on ahead, Arline," he said. "It's almost tea time, and one late-comer will be enough. I'll string the fish and follow you in a jiffy."

"Don't be long," Arline said, as she made her way up the steps to the roadway.

In spite of the fact that it was almost tea time she went rather slowly up the lane and turned in at the silvered gates of "Thatchwell." She found herself wondering if her aunt had seen Mrs. McCallum-Blair and—with quickening heart-beats—if there would be any news of Gavin.

She took the nearest way to the drawing-room where she expected to find her aunt and Helen, and passed by the "circular tour" through the kitchen and morning-room to the dining-room beyond.

Pausing at the mirror above the morning-room mantelpiece to smooth her hair, she became aware of a murmur of voices in the dining-room. Subconsciously she recognised Helen's low tones, though she could not make out the words. The door between the two rooms was slightly ajar, and when Mrs. Penner's voice took up the conversation, she might have been speaking in the same room.

"You have always been ready to champion Arline, I know, Helen," she said, "but this is quite a different matter."

In spite of herself, Arline's progress towards the dining-room was arrested.

"But I don't believe it!" Helen was protesting in a louder tone now. "Gavin would never do such a thing."

Mrs. Penner's harsh laugh rang out.

"You can scarcely upbraid him for it, Helen," she said. "After all, it was a gentleman's only way out."

"But Arline? It can't be true. He proposed to her—he told her he was in love with her." Helen's voice held the suspicion of tears.

"Was there any other way?" her mother demanded. "He was only trying to make the best of things. I might say he was most considerate of her feelings, since such a marriage can never have a romantic angle in the man's eyes. He knew of the gossip which was going about at Glen Solan, and he's done what he considered the right thing."

Arline's face had gone deathly pale. She felt as if the room was slowly closing in upon her until soon the walls would be crushing her—closer, closer. She put her hand up to her throat as if to tear off the iron band which seemed to be clamped there, while the drone of voices in the next room came, now loud, now fainter, fainter. . . .

With a desperate effort she pulled herself together. There was no thought in her mind of creeping from the scene the way she had come. With her head held high, she opened the dining-room door and stood confronting her aunt.

"Perhaps it would be better if I heard what is being said about me, Aunt Hilda."

119

Even in her distress, she was able to marvel at the calmness of her own voice. It held the chilliness of despair, had she been able to recognise the feeling at the moment, but she only knew that a terrible surging emotion was rising within her and that it was threatening to choke her. And yet she spoke calmly.

Mrs. Penner was quick to recover from her first surprise.

"Yes, perhaps it would be better," she said, "since you seem to be rather blind to all the signs."

Arline felt that she could not bear her aunt's usual preliminaries.

"Please make it as short and painless as possible," she said, her voice beginning to shake a little. "I think you hinted just now that my engagement was a matter of—of 'a gentleman's only way out.' Perhaps you will be good enough to tell me what you mean?"

"Mother . . !"

Helen, who would not have protested on her own behalf, took courage to intervene for her cousin.

"Don't interfere, Helen, if you please," Mrs. Penner said. "Arline has asked for the truth, and I'm afraid she must have it—much as I hate to repeat it." She turned back to Arline. "It seems to be quite common knowledge to everyone that Gavin Shandon is merely marrying you out of a sense of decency. There has been more gossip than even I imagined there would be at Glen Solan, and he obviously thinks it the right thing to do."

"It's not true!" Arline's voice was little more than a whisper. "I won't believe it. You're only saying this to try to hurt me!"

Mrs. Penner shrugged her shoulders.

"You don't seriously think a man in Gavin Shandon's position would *want* to marry a secretary," she said. "Not, at any rate, when he had other plans."

The shaft drove home.

"You mean—he wanted to marry someone else?" Arline could scarcely voice the question. "How do you know?"

"Need I remind you that I have just been to see his mother?"

The words seemed to be the final blow to Arline. She tried to speak, to answer that last, strangely convincing argument of her aunt's, but she could not. An almost tangible grey mist seemed to be enveloping her, wrapping her in its blinding folds. She groped for the door.

"What do you intend to do?"

The question seemed to come from a thousand miles away, but she recognised her aunt's voice, sharp with curiosity. She tried to answer calmly.

"I don't know. I can't think—yet." She turned and met the cold blue-eyed stare. "I can't stay here," she continued desperately. "I only know I can't stay here!"

III

All through that long, sleepless night Arline lay on her narrow bed, praying that sleep would come to dull the pain which throbbed in her heart. But her mind was too active: thoughts drove sleep from her, thoughts which swirled round in her brain in a fiery circle, lashing her with the scorn of her own pride.

How easy it was to see everything now! How blind—how unutterably blind—she had been before! She must not allow her heart to dictate to her; she must see this thing as it was, stripped of all illusion, as her aunt had presented it to her. Gavin had proposed to her, lied to her, because he felt that it was his duty to do so—because it was "a gentleman's only way out." He had pretended that he cared for her because he felt that it was the right thing to do, while all the time he was in love with someone else.

It was this one bitter fact which blinded her to all else in those first moments of wounded love and despair, and that the information had come from Gavin's mother made it doubly credible.

Her pride rose in revolt. She had been fool enough to believe him, to read into his love-making all that she had ever dreamed should be there.

That was another thing she would never forgive. He had made love to her so convincingly, he had been so gentle, so tender. . . .

Tears dimmed her eyes. She could not bear to think of it, and of how she had returned his caresses, and of all she had said in the moments of sweet confession. A hurt, wounded pride raised its head and demanded reparation.

Each time he had held her in his arms—kissed her—he had been thinking of someone else, longing to hold them, but knowing it impossible now. Oh, it was intolerable—even to think of it!

Burying her head in the pillows, she tried to marshal her thoughts to a line of action. If there had only been one way out for Gavin, there was one way out for her.

Incident after incident had been leading up to her departure from the Penner household for a very long time. This, then, was *her* way out! Strange how clearly the details formed in your mind even though your heart was dead within you. She must leave Winter's Quay at once. She would be gone when Gavin came back. She would go somewhere—to Glasgow, probably—and find some work to do that would at least make her independent. There was a little money still to her credit in the bank, and she must chance finding employment before that was done.

And Gavin?

Her heart contracted within her at the thought of him. She had lost him—lost him for ever.

What a fool to think of him like that! All the tenderly sweet things he had ever said were lies—a sham and a mockery. Pride, which should have no part in love, had its way.

She would not let him think that she cared; she would let him see that she, too, had been playing a game. She would give him his freedom to marry the woman he wanted.

Who was she?

Arline shook the thought from her. Why should she care who she was? It did not matter to her—now.

She lay back on her bed and stared at the grey oblong of the window. It was raining, slow, determined rain that seeped through the trees like difficult tears falling through gnarled fingers. Why should she think of tears? She had no place for them.

Rising, she drew the curtains back to let in the thin, grey streaks of the dawn. Noiselessly she moved about the room packing her belongings into the two suit cases she had brought with her. She had made up her mind to catch the early morning boat to Gourock, and had even thought out the hotel in Glasgow where she would book accommodation for a night or two.

In the room next door the maids were stirring. Arline sat down at the table beside the window and wrote two letters. One she would leave on the morning-room mantelpiece for Mrs. Penner, and the other, addressed to Gavin at Rowan Gate, she would take with her when she left and post it in Glasgow.

The morning rolls had arrived, and Alice boiled her some hot milk before Nellie Anderson put in an appearance in the kitchen to prepare the breakfast.

It had been a difficult half-hour for Arline, and she heaved a sigh of relief as she heard the heavy gate of "Thatchwell" clang behind her for the last time. She knew that her aunt would brand her departure as selfish and ungrateful, but she could not help that. She had felt that she could not bear the ordeal of saying good-bye to Helen and Dougie with Mrs. Penner looking on, and perhaps another scene to face before she left.

The streets of Glasgow were thronged with the business crowd when she stepped out of the Central Station and made her way to the hotel in the quiet square off Bath Street where she had once stayed for a week with her father.

It took little time to settle in and instruct the porter to have her suit cases collected from the station where she had left them. A kindly waitress asked if she would like breakfast, but Arline shook her head. She had no desire for food nor, in spite of the sleepless night behind her, did she want to rest. She felt that she must do something, get about somewhere, so that she might not think.

It was not quite half-past ten when she turned into Sauchiehall Street and wandered along trying to concentrate on the shop windows and the crowd of gay, chattering women who thronged the pavements at this fashionable shopping hour.

They haven't a care in the world, she thought, looking from one group to another: meeting friends for coffee on a Saturday morning—so many friends! Why were her thoughts so bitter? She had all her life before her to make friends, she told herself, but in her heart she knew that all the friendships in the world would never make up to her for the loss of Gavin Shandon. Even though she knew he had never cared for her, there would never be anyone else.

She walked on slowly, looking in windows, seeing his face against the black velvet hangings of an art store, his grey eyes looking out at her as she gazed at the blooms in a florist's, the thought of his ring lying in her bag when she stopped before a jeweller's.

Choosing a restaurant at random, she went in and ordered a coffee and biscuits, which she left lying untouched on the table before her.

"Now, I'm sure it is! I've been wondering if I was right ever since you came in."

The deep, Canadian drawl sounded at her elbow, and Arline glanced up, startled out of her reverie.

"Arline Hamilton, isn't it?"

"Martin Lang?"

The name formed haltingly on Arline's lips. She could scarcely reconcile this giant of a man with the slim boy who had been her music teacher's son. Yet, the features were unmistakable, and the tawny hair that no amount of attention could ever control.

"The same! Imagine you remembering." Lang sat down on the vacant seat beside her. "You don't mind, do you?" he asked. "I guess you're sorta by yourself."

"Yes," Arline admitted.

"Then, that's fine," Lang declared, waving the waitress over. "What will you have?"

"Nothing more, thank you," Arline said. "I'm not really hungry. I just came in—out of the crowd."

"So did I, but I was beginning to think that I had brought the crowd in with me when I spotted you," Lang replied. "You're sure you won't have something else?"

"No thanks, really."

Martin Lang did not persist. He was studying her closely, and behind his bluff manner other thoughts were stirring. When his own coffee had been brought, he asked conversationally:

"What are you doing with yourself these days? Are you still as keen on the piano? I can remember when you were my mother's star pupil."

"I still play, of course," Arline admitted, "though I haven't had any tuition since—since my father died."

"Oh, I'm sorry to hear about that," Lang said with ready sympathy. "Was it long ago, or just sort of recent?"

"Four years ago," Arline told him, feeling that it had been only yesterday.

This meeting with Martin was bringing the past back so vividly—the pleasant years when she had only had her music to think of, and all the world had been young and gay with so much to conquer. She remembered how she had planned a musical career so light-heartedly before the crash had come and there had been no money left to pave the way for that career. Martin had been young then, too. She visioned him as the long-legged youth who had teased her because her exercises had always been completed in time, her practice done with a will and her theory perfect. His mother had been one of the best-known teachers of the pianoforte in the city, and she had been proud of Arline as a pupil.

"How is your mother—and Kathie?" Arline asked.

"Mother died two years ago," Lang said, his face suddenly grave. "A stroke, followed by a quick and merciful release. I was in Canada at the time, and she was dead before I could get over. I wanted Kathie to come back with me, but I couldn't persuade her. She had started a place of her own here—she went in for dancing, you remember? — and it was just beginning to get on its feet, so she wouldn't throw it up. Now, it's a roaring success."

"Kathie's not—Kay Lang?" Arline asked quickly, the light of interest in her eyes for a moment.

"The same," Martin acknowledged with obvious pride. "I'll admit she's made good in a great big way."

"She certainly has," Arline replied. "And you?" she asked.

"I've just come over to the old country for a long rest," he replied. "My first in six years. I always fancied farming, you know, and my mother put some money into a ranch in Canada for me. I own the place now since the other fellow died," he continued, with some pride in his achievement. "I've made good, but I've worked hard for it—too hard, my doctor insists, though he has to admit there isn't a loose nut anywhere in my tough framework."

Arline smiled at his straightforward admissions. He was

quite different from the Martin Lang she remembered.

"All the same," he went on, "I argued myself into this holiday at last—and here I am." He smiled across at her. "Now, what about you? Where have you been and what have you been doing with yourself? You look all washed-up," he added frankly but kindly.

Arline did not want to speak about herself. She gave him the briefest details.

"I went to live with an uncle after my father died," she said. "I don't think there's an awful lot to tell. There hasn't been anything very exciting—not anything interesting."

"You're still living in Glasgow, then?" Lang asked.

"Yes."

"Now, thats all right." She saw him glance at her left hand. "Not married or anything?" he asked bluntly.

"No—not anything," she replied, breaking a biscuit nervously on her plate.

She liked Martin Lang, but she wished at the moment that she had not stumbled upon him like this. She felt that she had not had time to gather her forces sufficiently to meet such a friendly and obviously interested attack.

"Are you still with this uncle?" Lang asked, at last, and Arline, driven to reply, could only tell him the truth.

"No, I—left this morning," she admitted, looking fixedly at the crushed biscuit on her plate. "I've come up to town to—to try and find work."

"I see," he said, "you just couldn't hit it off with your folks. Well, I don't blame you for cutting adrift. Relations can be the very devil sometimes."

"I'm afraid that it was—the last of many misunderstandings that forced me away to-day," she said, conscious that it was beginning to be something of a relief to talk to somebody who was not ready to misjudge her.

Lang was making a series of mental notes as she spoke, and his shrewd brown eyes seemed to take in the whole situation at a glance. She's all wrought-up, he thought, and these damned relations of hers have been worrying her until she's cut out on her own to look for a job she might not land for months. There's something else, too, but I can't just put my finger on it—yet.

"Well, he said to Arline, "and when does the big onslaught on the labour market begin?"

She was forced to laugh.

"I mean to start looking round for work on Monday," she said. "I'll get the *Herald* and answer a few advertisments to-night."

"What?" Lang smiled. "On a Saturday? It's half day here, isn't it? Why not come along to Helensburgh with me and meet Kathie? She'll be real glad to see you again."

Though Kathie Lang and she had been very good friends in the old days, Arline found herself making excuses, excuses she knew that Martin must see through immediately, but she felt that she could not accept his invitation to-day. She had come into the crowded restaurant to escape from herself and now, perversely, she wanted to be alone. It was possible that he might be offended, but she felt that she could not help herself.

Lang, however, was not offended. Her stumbling excuses had only added to his conviction that everything was far from right with Arline Hamilton, the girl whose memory had clung to him through six years of struggle and success.

"I guess you want to get settled in at your new digs," he said. "I'll give you a day or two, and then you must look Kathie up."

"I'd like to do that," Arline said. "In a day or two."

He accompanied her back to the hotel and left her at the foot of the flight of stone steps which led up to the door.

"I'm going to call round on Tuesday afternoon and see how you're getting along," he said. "You'll let me do that?"

Arline could not refuse. He had been kind, and he and Kathie were a link with the past when she had been young and happy and her father had been her close companion.

IV

The postman dropped the knocker on the oak door of Rowan Gate and waited.

"Registered letter, Bessie," he said conversationally, when a maid had appeared in answer to his summons. "For Mr. Gavin Shandon—frae Glasgow."

The maid regarded him stonily.

"Well, an' what of it, Donal' McNeish?" she demanded tartly. "Show me where to sign ma name an' I'll be gettin' about ma business."

"Indeed, then! Sign there." McNeish was nettled. "Some folks are aye gettin' up oot o' the rang side o' the bed in the mornin', I'm thinkin'."

Bessie signed her name and handed back his pencil without a word. The door of Rowan Gate closed again.

"Bletherin' old fool!" Bessie remarked to the hallway as she carried the letter into the lounge. "Somethin' for you, Mr. Gavin," she announced.

Gavin Shandon swung round from the window. He took the letter in his hand, but he did not attempt to open it for a very long time. He stood there gazing down at the blue lines on the registered envelope as if he could read through them the message which lay inside. His face was almost devoid of expression: only his teeth biting savagely into the stem of his pipe gave any indication of his feelings. He knew what the package contained. He had been to see Mrs. Penner the day before.

Slowly and deliberately he tore it open at last, shaking the ring into the palm of his hand. The diamonds lay winking up at him in the bright morning light, but he did not seem to see them. Thrusting it into the pocket of his jacket, he extracted the single sheet of notepaper and read the few brief lines Arline had penned at the height of her grief and disappointment. They had been dictated by a hurt pride which strove to hurt him in return.

"Dear Gavin,

"I am sending you back your ring, and I hope you will release me from any promise I may have made. I have discovered that the whole thing was a ghastly mistake leading out of a most unusual situation. I should never have mistaken it for love, and now that I realise my error I ask you for my freedom, believing that this is the best way.

"Please don't try to see me or trace me. Nothing could persuade me to change my mind.

"Yours very sincerely,
"Arline Hamilton."

His face was almost grey as he stared down at her name: he was like a figure carved in granite. The stillness of the room was accentuated by the very immobility of the man who stood within its quiet walls remembering the day on the Firth of Lorne when a girl in a disabled boat had drifted across his horizon. Outside birds were clamouring in the ivy, and in the distance a dog was barking incessantly.

At last he moved, walking down the full length of the long room. When he turned his heel ground into the soft depth of the carpet. Very deliberately he produced another letter from the inside pocket of his jacket, and, smoothing it out, read it over slowly. When he had finished his mouth relaxed in a grim smile. He took both letters and crushed them slowly in his hand.

"She wrote them both—within a week," he said aloud.

A laugh which was hardly mirthful broke into the silence of the room.

Turning, he moved slowly to the window, his hands thrust deep in the pockets of his jacket. The sound of barking outside was drawing nearer, and there was the crunch of a light footstep on the gravel beneath the open window. He looked down into the hazel eyes of his step-sister.

"Why the dark frown on such a glorious morning?" Sheena McCallum-Blair asked lightly, bending down to take the barking terrier in her arms and so silence him.

Shandon made no reply to her question. Instead he countered with another.

"What have you been doing all morning?"

Sheena smiled frankly.

"It was going to be quite a secret, but I don't suppose I'd have the heart to keep it from you. Come and see," she invited eagerly.

For a moment Shandon hesitated, and then, with a shrug, he swung his legs over the low window-sill and jumped the short distance to the gravel beneath.

Sheena led the way round the end of the house and through the shrubbery to a small, creeper-covered shed at the far side, which had never been used since the McCallum-Blairs had bought Rowan Gate. Gavin remembered it as a haunt of spiders whose propriety rights had never been disputed. Sheena unlocked the door.

"You can come in," she said. "There are no spiders now."

Shandon bent his head and entered. The place had been swept and scrubbed and dusted until it shone. Originally it had been a well-constructed little hut with a sound, teak floor, every inch of which had been polished until it glistened. An ancient, damp-marked mirror in a tarnished gilt frame had been propped against one wall, and along the other was a short handrail which had been built into the shed for some purpose best known to the original owner. It did not need the pair of well-worn ballet shoes which lay on the floor to acquaint Shandon with the new purpose of this strange little room among the shrubs. There was something infinitely touching about the pains Sheena had taken to make herself a practice room even at Rowan Gate.

"You're very keen, aren't you, Sheena?" he said at last. "Does mother know about your hide-away?"

"No, not yet," Sheena admitted. "I didn't want to trouble her while she was ill."

Shandon turned from his contemplation of the blurred mirror.

"This sort of thing means a lot to you?" he asked.

"Everything, Gavin!" she replied earnestly. "I live for dancing."

"And you're going to be a very disappointed young woman if you are not allowed to go on with it?"

Her smiling eyes clouded over.

"Nothing else would ever hold my enthusiasm. If I can't go back for tuition in the autumn I don't really mind what happens."

"I see," Shandon said, turning back along the shrubbery path. "Look here, Sheena, would you like me to put the facts to your father?"

"Would you? Oh, Gavin, would you?"

He smiled down at her for an instant.

"Why not?" he said. "It won't do any harm, if it does no good."

She clasped his arm impulsively.

"You're a brick!" she cried. "If anyone can convince dad, you can. Oh, if I can only go back. . . ."

He disengaged her clinging fingers and gave them an encouraging pat.

"Keep up the practice, and I'll see what I can do when I come back," he promised.

"Oh, you're going away?"

"Yes, for a week or two. I have rather urgent business which will keep me in London until September, but I'll do my best to see your dad before I go."

"The first quarter starts in September," Sheena reminded him.

"All right, youngster!" Don't worry, I'll try to see him to-morrow," he promised.

"Oh, if you would. . . !"

She gave his hand a grateful squeeze, and, calling Jock, was off down the narrow path to the shore.

Shandon turned slowly back towards the shrubbery, where the gardener had lit a smouldering fire earlier in the day. His hand clenched round the two letters he had crushed into his pocket in the lounge. He drew them out and tore them across and across. Then, very deliberately, he threw the pieces one by one on to the fire.

CHAPTER EIGHT

THE BOND OF FRIENDSHIP

I

EVEN within two short days Arline was beginning to realise just how difficult it is to obtain employment without the necessary qualifications. Although she had a good many years of practical experience behind her she had never attended any of the recognised schools, nor did she hold any certificates for secretarial work.

Well, it was only two days, she tried to reason with herself on the afternoon of the Tuesday, and something was bound to turn up sooner or later. If she could not find a secretarial post, she must look round for something else.

There was a discreet tap on her bedroom door.

"Come in," Arline called, and the little chambermaid who had shown her up that first morning came round the door.

"There's a gentleman down in the lounge would like to see you, Miss Hamilton," she said.

Arline rose swiftly to her feet, all the colour draining from her face. Gavin Shandon's name had rushed to her mind.

"He said you'd be expecting him, miss."

"Oh, yes," Arline turned to the mirror over the small wash-basin. "Thank you. Will you tell Mr. Lang I'll be down in a few minutes, please?"

Lang was standing at one of the long windows which overlooked the street, and he whirled round quickly as she entered.

"Well, here I am—as promised," he said cheerfully. "Who's secretary are you now?"

Arline shook hands.

"I'm afraid I'm still on the market," she replied. "Nobody seem to realise what is being offered to them!"

It was impossible to be disheartened with Martin Lang about. He dispelled gloom as the sunshine dispels the wisps of cloud after rain.

"That may have its advantages," he said, his brown eyes twinkling, "but we're not going into that now. Step up to the window a moment. There's something out there I want you to run your eye over."

He led Arline to the window and drew back the curtain so that she might see out. A long, low-slung car was drawn up at the kerb in front of the hotel, and a passing boy was examining the dashboard with grave interest.

"What do you think of her?" Lang queried.

"Very nice. Is it yours?" Arline asked. "It—it looks very superior."

"Well, that's saying something," Lang laughed. "Come on out and let me show you her paces."

Arline hesitated.

"I should be doing some more job-hunting this afternoon," she objected.

"There are other days," Lang assured her philosophically. "It's too fine to stay in town to-day. Say you'll come."

Why not? It was a glorious day, and she was lonely and tired and just a little dispirited.

"Where would you like to go?" he asked, when they were seated in the new car.

"Anywhere. I'm not particular," Arline replied, settling down in the comfortable leather well of the seat.

It was perhaps an unfortunate coincidence that Martin Lang chose the road to Loch Lomond and took the Rowardennan side of the loch. It plunged Arline deep into a vortex of memories that made her strangely silent throughout the short run. Lang, however, kept up a flow of conversation about his life in Canada and, if he noticed her silence, he did not comment upon it.

Time after time Arline drew her thoughts back to the conversation to make some fitting reply to his remarks, but soon they would revert again to that other drive along these self-same roads with Helen, and from there they would journey on the dangerous pathway of bitter-sweet memory. She had thought so often of Helen during the past few days, and now she remembered the conversation they had had that day when they had driven out in the Daimler in search of a refreshing breeze. Lang's car had taken them almost to the spot where Helen and she had lain on the grass and gazed up at the benignant curve of old Ben

Lomond etched against the sky. She remembered how they had discussed pride, and how she had told Helen that she thought all kinds of pride were much the same, and all of them equally futile. Had some perverse fate sought to prove her wrong?

When they were approaching Glasgow on the return journey, she told Lang that she thought she had made a very listless companion, but he smiled rather slowly and said:

"I talk enough for two."

They were going slowly along the broad stretch of the Great Western Road, and he added abruptly:

"I promised Kathie to bring you back to tea. You'll come, won't you? She's sure anxious to see you again."

"Is she in Glasgow?" Arline asked.

"Yes. She would have come along to meet you this afternoon, but the poor kid's up to the eyes in work," Lang explained. "She's taken over a new place. At first she had rooms in the Majestic at Charing Cross, but the management wanted double their price this season, so she decided to fix up a place of her own."

"Perhaps I shouldn't trouble her yet," Arline said. "She must be very busy."

"She expressly told me to bring you along." Lang would take no refusal, and already he was turning the car down towards Charing Cross. "The place is still in a bit of an upset, but Kathie's got her own quarters all fixed up. She's expecting us, so you can't let me down."

Arline gave in.

"All right," she said, "I'll come."

She was quite anxious to meet Kathie Lang again, she realised, as they turned into one of the quieter streets and drew up before a large, substantial house which had recently been painted. A plate on the railings proclaimed it to be "Kay Lang's Dancing Academy, Fenmore House."

Before they had reached the door it was flung open and Kathie came out on the top step to greet them.

"I heard the car and saw you from the ball-room window," she said, taking both Arline's hands in hers, and gazing at her with frank and friendly curiosity. "Why, Arline, you're not so very much changed in all these years! How are you?"

"Very well, thanks," Arline answered, allowing herself to be drawn into the big square hall.

"You'll have to excuse the bareness of it all," Kathie went on, waving her expressive little hands towards the carpetless stairway, "but I haven't got properly fixed up yet, and the tradesmen are being very trying. Either that, or I haven't got a business head."

She lead the way up the broad staircase to the second floor. There was a vague sound of hammering on the premises, and odd pieces of furniture were stacked outside some of the doors.

"The men are still busy with the public rooms," Kathie explained. "I'm having the ball-room floor relaid, and the rest of the place decorated, but I'm beginning to fear that it will never be ready by September."

"Of course it will be ready," her brother assured her. "And whether it is or not, you've to take that holiday I prescribed before you face a winter's work."

Kathie smiled up at Arline.

"Isn't he a tyrant? I don't know how I ever managed to build up this business without him!"

The passage ended in a smooth, cream enamelled door which swung open to admit them to Kathie's living-quarters. Here everything was in order, and the tiny flat, tucked away from the rest of the house behind its cream door, was a homely place which reflected its owner's personality.

"Come into the lounge," Kathie invited, "I've set tea in there so that we can be cosy and have a nice long chat afterwards."

Arline scarcely knew what they spoke of in that first hour. It seemed that Kathie and she had lifted the threads of their old friendship just where they had dropped them, and as if it had been yesterday. There was no need to "break the ice," for there was no ice and no false pride about Kathie Lang. She welcomed Arline quite frankly as a person whose friendship she had missed more than a little in the years when she had been struggling to build up her connection, and she confessed that she had had no time to form other friendships.

"I wish we had met sooner, Arline," she said, when Martin had pushed the tea table out of their way and they had gathered round the fire, "but I don't mean to let you slip away a second time." She turned to her brother. "Have you asked Arline yet?" she questioned.

Lang shook his head.

"I was leaving that to you."

Kathie ran her hand over the smooth raven-black wings of her hair in a little gesture which was characteristic of her when she was about to approach a delicate situation.

"Arline," she began. "are you definitely set on getting secretarial work?"

"If I possibly can," Arline replied. "You see," she went on to explain, "it's the only thing I can do."

Kathie bent forward in her chair.

"What about your music?" she asked. "Have you never thought of using that?"

Arline was puzzled.

"In what way, Kathie?"

"Well, it's like this." Kathie spread out her hands. "I'm stuck for a pianist and—well, will you help me out? Will you take the job?"

Arline drew a deep breath while she looked slowly from Kathie to her brother. The expression on Martin's face told her plainly that he would be more than ordinarily disappointed if she refused this offer. Arline wondered from whom the suggestion had come originally, but even as she wondered she felt heartily grateful to Kathie for the way in which she had framed the offer. She knew that Kay Lang had only to advertise for a pianist in any local newspaper to receive more replies than she could possibly consider.

"I'd love to take it, Kathie," she said, at last, "but is it fair to you?"

Kathie looked surprised.

"I mean—aren't you taking a big risk?" Arline went on. "I've never played in public before, far less for a dancing class like yours. I don't know the first thing about it."

"There's really very little to know," Kathie assured her with a smile, "and what little there is you can easily learn before the classes begin in September. I know you have a perfect sense of time and rhythm. That's about all you need, so if you think you can put up with me shouting at you from time to time, the only other attribute you must have is an unlimited fund of patience."

Arline smiled.

"Do you think I could do it?" she asked, hesitating before giving her final reply.

"Of course you can," Kathie declared. "I've told you there's very little in it, and I take it you'll be willing to practise?"

"Oh, yes! Just as much as you like," Arline cried. "Kathie—this is awfully good of you—I can't begin to thank you."

"Don't," Kathie laughed. "You might feel like taking it all back once you've seen me at work. I'm terribly exacting, you know."

"I'd rather have it that way," Arline declared.

"There's something else," Kathie said.

"Yes?"

"Well, I told you I hadn't a head for figures, and there's all this business of taking over the house. I loathe bills and settling with tradesmen when I should be planning a new ballet for the season." Kathie came over and sat down on the divan at Arline's side. "Could you take over that responsibility for me right now?" she asked.

A ridiculous lump rose in Arline's throat.

"Thank you," she said rather breathlessly. "When shall I begin?"

"The sooner the better, I think. Kathie is in a definite fix with all these details, and she'll only end by getting in deeper and deeper."

Martin, who had been strangely quiet during the discussion, came forward and, snapping open a case, offered them a cigarette. There was a gleam of satisfaction in his brown eyes as he glanced down at Arline.

"Really, he's right," Kathie admitted. "I'm not at all commercially inclined. So, shall we say that's settled, Arline? You start work here next Monday. Is that sufficient warning?"

"Quite," Arline assured her, and going back in the car to Bath Street, she tried to thank Martin for all they had done for her.

"Shucks! That's nothing," he replied. "It's a poor guy who can't help a friend. Besides, Kathie needed a secretary about as much as she needed a pianist."

II

When Arline looked back on the weeks which followed that first visit to Fenmore House, she was glad from the bottom of her heart that her days had been almost too full to permit of thought. The secretarial work came easy to her, and soon she had Kathie's affairs well in hand, leaving her friend to attend to the dancing routines for the new season. There had been so much to do, but Arline had put every ounce of concentration and energy of which she was capable into her work, feeling that in this way she could best forget the past.

August passed almost unnoticed, and by the beginning of September Kathie pronounced herself satisfied with all they had accomplished in so short a time.

"I believe I'll even have time to take that week's rest Martin ordered," she said to Arline one evening, as they stood in the empty ball-room surveying the fruits of their labours. "To tell you the truth, I think I'd feel much better for a change of scenery before I begin the winter's work in earnest."

"Where will you go?" Arline asked.

"Down to Helensburgh, I expect," Kathie replied. It's quiet there, and there's no great distance to travel. Since I can only spare myself a week, travelling is a consideration."

"Do try to go, Kathie," Arline advised, noting the fine lines of fatigue at the corners of her friend's eyes. "I'll look after things until you come back."

"There isn't a great deal to do," Kathie said. "I'm booked up now, and I can't take one extra pupil if I mean to do justice to the others." She turned away towards the hall. "There's just one other thing, Arline," she continued. "I know you're comfortable enough at that hotel of yours, but it would save an awful lot of time and running back and forward if you digged in with me. There's a bedroom upstairs simply crying out to be occupied, and it would be good company for both of us. What do you say?"

Arline did not take long to consider. Though she was comfortable enough at the hotel, she had come to look upon Kathie's little flat as home—the first time she had felt like applying that word to a house for many years.

Kathie arranged that she should move in almost immediately, and so, a few days before his sister left for Helensburgh for her well-earned holiday, Martin called at the hotel and took Arline and her suit-cases to Fenmore House.

"You won't be lonely here," Kathie told her. "There's the maid and Burt, the caretaker, and his wife on the premises, and Martin has promised to bring you down to Helensburgh to see me one evening, so the week will soon go in."

It passed even quicker than Arline had anticipated. A last-minute desire to join Kay Lang's exclusive dancing classes seemed to have spread through the West End of Glasgow. Everyone who was anyone, and also had a daughter between the ages of four and sixteen, was obviously possessed by the desire to see her a pupil of Kay Lang's.

On the Wednesday morning she was opening a batch of these letters when the signature at the foot of one sheet of notepaper caught her eye. The request was signed "Evelyne McCallum-Blair," and Arline glanced quickly at the address. Yes, it had been sent from Rowan Gate. She laid it down on the desk before her and stared out of the window.

In spirit she was miles away on the sunny slope of the hill above Loch Solan, and a girl in a tartan kilt was offering her the first of the rhododendron blossoms. Sheena McCallum-Blair's face rose before her vividly, and she remembered their conversation as if it had taken place yesterday. The girl was eager to dance, and her mother had frowned upon the idea. That was the impression Arline had obtained during their short talk. She wondered what had made Mrs. McCallum-Blair change her mind.

And then other memories came flooding in upon her, memories that she had foolishly believed she could lock out of her heart for ever. They took her unawares, so that her head went down on her hands on the crushed letter, and she sobbed his name at last.

"Gavin—oh, Gavin. . . !"

When she raised her head her eyes were dry, but there was a shadow in them that was deeper than tears.

She answered the letter as she had done the other requests that had been too late, but she thought of Sheena McCallum-Blair with a little twinge of compassion.

That evening Martin called at Fenmore House to take Arline on the promised visit to his sister. As they drove along the almost deserted roads, with the autumn hedgerows fresh and sweet after a shower of rain, Arline thought how rapidly their friendship had developed in so short a space of time. Perhaps it had been the sure bond of work shared that had drawn them together, and, of course, they had not started as strangers.

Some such thoughts must have been stirring in Lang's mind, too, for, as they neared their destination and the car was purring slowly through Cardross village, he said:

"We seem to have known each other a good deal longer than six weeks, Arline. It makes me feel as if the years I spent abroad were just a dream—a pleasant and interesting dream, I admit, but holding nothing of reality, if you get what I mean?"

"I think I do," Arline replied slowly, her thoughts wavering back to all those years had held for her.

Was that a dream, too, holding nothing of reality, as Martin had expressed it? Yes, that was how she must think of it now.

"It's lonely where I come from," Lang went on, "but I've come to think of it as home. When a man puts everything into the soil, it has claimed him for all time."

"You'll be going back soon?" Arline asked, with a vague consciousness that she would miss his companionship.

"I've two months, yet," he said, turning from the wheel to look at her. "It doesn't seem enough now, and when I first arrived I thought the time would never pass."

"You've been kept busy most of your holiday," Arline reminded him.

"I haven't minded that," he replied, "and its given me your friendship."

There was a vibrating note in his pleasant voice as he made the confession, and the colour rose in Arline's cheeks as she heard it. Her hand was lying loosely over her bag, and suddenly he covered it with his own and gave it a gentle squeeze.

"Arline, I can't expect you to care all this quickly, but I want you to know that this is no new feeling with me. I've cared for you for a very long time—and I always will," he said.

Kathie was at the gate of the cottage to meet them, and Arline greeted her with a quickly beating heart. There was so much to tell Kathie, and yet, all through their conversation, Martin Lang's words were echoing in her ears. She knew that she had thought of Martin solely as a kind and interesting friend; there had never been anything else in her mind, and his confession in the car had come as something of a shock to her. All along he had treated her as he had treated Kathie, in a generous, big-brotherly way, ordering them both about when he thought that they were overworking, and admonishing Arline as readily as he reproved his sister. He had been someone big and substantial to turn to in an emergency, for Arline as well as Kathie. They had both taken him very much for granted, and now, Arline thought, it could never be quite the same again.

It was late before they finished tea and, as there was only one bedroom in a little cottage, Martin went out to find accommodation in a nearby hotel.

"We'll have a walk before we go to bed," Kathie suggested. "Martin seems to have got into conversation with the locals at his hotel."

It was a clear, starry night, with a little breeze straying in from the Gareloch, and they walked rapidly along the promenade. There was nothing in the appearance of the night that should have made Arline think of Glen Solan and the incident on the island, but her thoughts reverted back to that misty evening and the placid waters of the loch before them became the turbulent expanse of the Lorne Firth. Vividly in her mind's eye she could see the two islands and the widening stretch of water that had grown between them as the tide came in, and Gavin standing on the far shore waiting for the dawn. As if they were symbolical, the waters seemed to rise and widen until they enveloped the islands in a rush and roar of waves.

Arline shivered involuntarily. The tide of circumstances and misunderstanding that now flowed between Gavin

141

and herself was as wide and as deep as that rushing channel between the islands.

Kathie turned at the end of the promenade.

"I think we'd better get back now," she said. "It will be fairly late before we get in."

Roused out of her reverie, Arline tried to keep up a flow of light conversation on the way back. Kathie, however, had noted her preoccupation, but she thought it wiser to say nothing about it at the moment. She considered that the time would come when Arline would confide her trouble in her of her own accord.

III

The following afternoon it was raining heavily when Martin brought the car round, and during the journey back to Glasgow they were forced to travel with the side windows tightly shut.

Arline could not help feeling a little quickening sense of embarrassment as they journeyed on in comparative silence. She found herself wishing with all her heart that Martin had not made his confession, and that they were back again on the easy footing of comradeship which had helped to brighten those first long weeks for her.

Martin did not refer to the subject again; it was as if he knew that Arline could not return his feelings for her yet, but something about the very fact that he left the subject closed seemed to suggest that he felt that time might yet prove a deciding factor in his favour.

"I'll pick you up to-morrow night at seven o'clock," he said, as he helped her out at Fenmore House. "You'll still come to the show, Arline?"

"Yes." She did not look up at him. "I'll be ready," she called, as she ran up the steps and pressed the bell.

A trim maid in a brown uniform and cream cap and apron opened the door.

"You got my telegram all right, I expect, Milly?" Arline asked, drawing off her gloves. "Anything important happened since I've been away?"

"Just two ladies about fixing up for the classes, Miss Hamilton," Milly replied. "They left their card and I told them you'd be replying." The girl hesitated, and

Arline paused on the first step and looked back at her. "There's someone—a young lady—to see you, miss. She called an hour ago, and she said she didn't mind how long she had to wait, but she must see you."

"Where is she?" Arline asked, wondering who could want to see her thus urgently.

"I put her in your office, miss. There was a fire in there, and it was so wet outside."

"All right, Milly." Arline turned to ascend the stairs. "Did she give her name?"

"No, miss."

Helen's name flashed through Arline's mind. She had written to her cousin two days before for the first time since she had left Winter's Quay, telling Helen of her new job, and studiously avoiding any mention of Gavin Shandon or the past. She knew that Mrs. Penner would read the letter, and her pride had forced her to speak of her new friends, Kay and Martin Lang, at great length. Perhaps the Penners had returned to town, and Helen had taken this opportunity to seek her out.

Arline paused with her hand on the knob of the office door, a smile of anticipation curving her lips. Her expression changed to one of genuine surprise, however, when she saw her visitor.

Sheena McCallum-Blair rose from the chair by the fire. "Good afternoon," she began. "Oh!"

Her surprise was even greater than Arline's, but the expression of incredulity was swiftly replaced by one of genuine pleasure.

"Why, it's you!" she cried. "I had no idea. Oh, this is splendid!"

Arline went forward and took the girl's outstretched hand. She had been strangely attracted by Sheena McCallum-Blair from the very first moment of their meeting in Glen Solan, and the fact that the girl was Gavin Shandon's step-sister made no difference.

"You've come about my letter, I expect, Miss McCallum-Blair?" she said. "You can imagine how sorry I was to have to refuse your request."

The smile faded from the girl's face.

"You mean—there *really* isn't a chance? I'm too late?"

Arline indicated the chair by the fire.

"Won't you sit down again?" she invited, and Sheena sank back into the deep chair, a small, almost forlorn figure in its capacious depths.

"I never dreamed I'd be too late," she said miserably, "and Gavin managed everything so nicely with dad, too." She looked up at Arline, explaining: "Gavin is my brother. Nobody could have talked dad round—or mums either, for that matter—but Gavin. Oh, Miss Hamilton, is it really no use asking again?"

Suddenly Arline made up her mind. She rose and pressed the bell on her desk, smiling down at her visitor.

"I think what we both need is a cup of tea," she said, "and—well, I'll tell Miss Lang she'd be very foolish to lose such an enthusiastic pupil."

"You will?" Sheena had sprung to her feet, her eyes shining. "Oh, Miss Hamilton! Oh, how can I ever, ever thank you?"

"I haven't made a definite promise that you'll be accepted, you know," Arline warned.

"Oh, but I know Miss Lang will listen to you," Sheena declared eagerly. "I couldn't bear to switch over to another teacher now; I've grown up with her methods."

Milly brought in the tea-tray and set it on the round Indian table beside Arline.

"Sugar and cream?"

"A very little sugar, but heaps of cream, thanks." Sheena sat down on the edge of the big chair again and accepted her cup. She studied Arline quite frankly. "I didn't see you at Glen Solan again," she went on. "I suppose you went away soon afterwards?"

"Yes."

Arline kept her eyes on her cup. It was inevitable that the conversation should come round to Glen Solan, but, somehow, she must change it to a less painful subject. Glen Solan and Gavin. She dare not think of that.

"We went away soon after that, too," Sheena explained, unconsciously ruthless. "Dad and Gavin are awfully keen on racing, and we have a house at Winter's Quay. Have you ever been to Winter's Quay, Miss Hamilton?"

Arline could no longer avoid the frank eyes opposite, and, as she looked across at Sheena, something of what she was feeling must have been in her expression, for the girl stopped abruptly and said:

"Oh, have I said anything to upset you?"

Arline forced a smile.

"No, nothing really." She got up and stood leaning on the low mantelpiece. "It's just that Winter's Quay has rather unpleasant memories for me, but you were not to know that."

"I'm sorry," Sheena said, and, with an effort to change the subject while she was drawing on her gloves, "We came up to town this morning. Mother is expecting Gavin back from London at the end of the week, and she wanted to be all settled in at home before he arrives."

So Gavin had been away—in London—all this time. Was there a chance that he had never received her letter? Arline's heart beat madly for a moment and then slowed up with a deliberation which she could almost feel. What room had she for such thoughts?

Sheena was thanking her again on her way to the door where Milly was waiting to show her downstairs, and Arline heard herself promising once more to speak to Kathie on her behalf. She watched Sheena go, realising that by her promise to the girl she had forged a link with the past she was trying so desperately to forget.

She approached Kathie about the matter almost immediately her friend returned from Helensburgh.

"Sheena McCallum-Blair?" Kathie murmured. "Good heavens, yes! I thought her name was a permanent fixture on my list. Of course you told her that it was quite all right?"

"I didn't know whether I could or not," Arline said. "I knew you were full up, and you said you couldn't make room for even one more."

"Sheena McCallum-Blair's different," Kathie replied. "There's no end of promise in that girl, and, quite frankly, I would hate to lose her as a pupil. Of course, I know that I will have to part with her some day if she means to go on with dancing as a career. She will have to go to one of the big masters."

"Then I can write to her and tell her that it is all right?"

Arline was surprised at the enthusiasm in her own voice. She was genuinely pleased that she had been able to help the girl.

And Sheena's gratitude was such that she would have done anything in her power to repay her.

IV

With the commencement of the dancing season Arline discovered a new and even more interesting Kathie Lang. Her friend threw herself heart and soul into the work, and gradually Arline began to feel the spell of it.

Their days were full, so full that they seldom left Fenmore House except for an odd shopping expedition into town or a short drive into the country with Martin. There were days, too, when things simply would not go right, and then Kathie would storm and rave in the little flat, and apologise as quickly as her mood had started.

"I can't keep sane when I have a bunch like that ballet class this morning," she would explain contritely over the cup of tea which Arline always prescribed. "Why do all fond mothers imagine that their offspring are embryo ballerinas?"

Arline would point out carefully that Kathie had one or two promising pupils, too.

"Where? Can you find them for me? There isn't one—with the exception of Sheena McCallum-Blair."

In these moods Arline called her Kay Lang, and Martin laughingly referred to his sister as The Lang.

Martin was indispensable to them. They relied upon him for what little amusement they had, and he was always cheerful. He was there, a solid background to their days, never too obtrusive, but edging his way slowly into Arline's life until he seemed to become part of it.

Sheena McCallum-Blair attended the advanced ballet classes twice a week. She mastered the routines quickly and often, when the others were going over steps again and again at the practice bar with Kathie, limp with despair, goading them on, Sheena would find her way across to the piano.

It was a strange friendship which grew between Arline and the girl, turning almost to worship on Sheena's part, and flourishing in spite of Arline's determination to curb it. Even the presence of Sheena in the class sent her vagrant thoughts down that forbidden pathway of memory: it was sheer madness to encourage her friendship, too. Yet, what could she do? Sheena herself was so sweet.

Towards the end of October Martin called at Fenmore House one bright morning and sat in the car pressing the horn to attract attention. Kathie and Arline were in the deserted ball-room going over a number for the class which would assemble in half an hour.

"There's Martin," Kathie said, following Arline to the window. "I wonder what he wants?"

She opened the heavy sash and looked out.

"Any chance of one of you coming for a run this fine morning?" Martin called up to them both, but he was looking at Arline as he made his request.

"You know I can't," Kathie replied, glancing at her watch. "I have a class in half an hour. You might persuade Arline, though."

"Could I, Arline?"

Arline turned to Kathie.

"Am I really no use?" she asked with a smile. "That's twice in one week that you've offered to do without me and use the recorder."

"You know it isn't that," Kathie replied. "It's only that I feel you're getting very little time to yourself and —well, Martin won't be here much longer, you know."

Something in her tone told Arline that she was aware of her brother's attachment and that she was desirous of furthering it.

"All the same," Arline said slowly, "I must do my job. Besides, we're going out with Martin to-night."

Martin pressed the self-starter until it gave out a vicious little exclamation which seemed expressive of his own thoughts.

"All right," he called back, as the car moved slowly forward, "I suppose work comes first, but don't forget I'm calling for you at seven-thirty."

Arline crossed the ball-room floor and, mounting the three steps to the platform, sat down at the piano and ran her fingers idly over the keys. Kay was still at the window, gazing out in the direction which her brother's car had taken. Arline stopped playing and looked across at her friend, while the silence between them seemed to grow and envelop the whole ball-room. At last Kathie came slowly down the room and sat on the edge of the platform.

"Arline," she said, "I'm not trying to interfere or force your confidence in any way, but—is there someone else?"

Arline's hands quivered over the keys and came down upon them in a wavering discord. For a moment a mist swam before her eyes so that black and white notes blurred together in an uneven line.

"You see," Kathie went on softly, "I can't help noticing how keen Martin is on you and—forgive me—how often you avoid him."

Arline made an effort to reply.

"I don't mean to be ungrateful," she said huskily. "Martin has been—very kind."

"Kind!" Kathie came up to the piano and leant her elbows on the flat top while she studied her friend. "What's troubling you, Arline?" she asked at last.

The genuine concern which lay behind the abrupt question pierced Arline's armour of reserve at last. In a rush and tumble of words which was an infinite relief to her mind she told Kathie the story of Glen Solan and all that had happened afterwards.

When she had finished there was a deep silence in the ball-room, but the tense atmosphere of conflicting thoughts had gone. Kathie spoke at last.

"You still care for Shandon, then?"

Arline looked down at the keyboard.

"I try to tell myself that I don't," she said.

"But it isn't much use, I suppose." Kathie turned and looked down the length of the room. "I know how you feel, dear, and it seems a little thing to say 'I'm sorry,' but I mean it from the bottom of my heart. But don't let it spoil your life, Arline. First love can be cruel, but there are other things—among them companionship and understanding."

Before Arline could find any reply the first pupils had appeared at the folding glass doors at the other end of the room. The class was a juvenile one, and the routines were simple and needed very little concentration on Arline's part. She stopped playing and started again at Kathie's commands almost automatically, while she went over in her mind the conversation just past.

It had been a great help to confide in her friend, and though she knew that Kathie must have received her confession with the thought of Martin ever in the background of her mind, it had been a relief to unburden her full heart. She had not thought it necessary to tell Kathie that Gavin was related to Sheena McCallum-Blair: in fact, she was trying to forget that relationship herself for her own peace of mind.

Martin was as punctual as ever, and he came in with a generous smile which bore no trace of his feelings of the morning.

As they drove through the busy streets, Arline studied the man by her side and wondered if she could ever bring herself to accept Kathie's proffered advice. First love *had* been cruel in her case, so cruel that the very thought of it had still power to wrench her heart and leave it quivering with pain. Was Kathie right? Were there other things in life that, in the end, might come to mean as much to her; things that could be had without pain and heartache? Friendship and a complete understanding. She could vision that with Martin.

"Here we are!" Kathie cried gaily, as they drove up at the entrance to the restaurant Martin had chosen. "It looks as if the place is going to be crowded to-night."

"Gustav Legrin is putting on a cabaret," Martin grinned at the delight his information caused. "I kept that up my sleeve as a surprise."

"Well, you've certainly surprised me," Kathie confessed. "I didn't even know he was in town. I'll have the time of my life trying to steal a few ideas."

Kay Lang was well known in the Q Restaurant, and they were conducted to their table by the head waiter, who presented the wine list to Martin and hovered behind his chair.

They had reached the coffee and liqueur stage before the lights dimmed and Gustav Legrin presented his cabaret. The applause was instantaneous, and as the lights went up again it rang out in wave after wave of appreciation.

"That was splendid, wasn't it?" Kathie cried, when it had died down.

A few dancers were taking the floor as the orchestra struck up a popular fox-trot.

"Why don't you two get up and dance?" Kathie suggested.

Martin rose and offered Arline his arm, and they began to pick their way through the tables to the cleared space in the centre of the room. Martin put his arm round her.

"Look," he said. "Kathie has company. Legrin has spotted her, and he's asking her to dance."

Arline looked over his shoulder and then her fingers tightened on her partner's arm, while her eyes met and were held by two steely grey ones across the room.

It seemed an eternity before Gavin Shandon bowed stiffly and turned back to his own table.

"What's the matter, Arline? Are you all right?"

Martin's voice seemed to splinter through glass before it reached her. With a great effort she pulled herself together.

"Yes—I'm all right. Shall we dance?"

The room was swaying round her and the music reached her, now loud, now soft. She forced herself to dance on, though her limbs felt numb and her feet seemed weighted with lead. She thought that the dance would never end, and wondered vaguely if Martin had spoken to her.

The music died away in a few soft bars, but there was an encore. She turned to Martin, and saw that his face was full of concern.

"Look here," he said. "Come and sit down. You look positively faint."

He led her back between the tables, and she thought that the tightness at her throat was going to choke her. Without looking in his direction, she was conscious of Gavin at his table in the far corner of the room. She knew that his eyes were upon her; she could almost feel their steady scrutiny.

"Can I get you something to drink?" Martin was asking. "It's this infernal heat. The place is like an oven to-night."

"I'm all right now, Martin," she said, and even managed a smile. "It *was* hot on the floor."

"We'll go," he said.

"No, Martin," Arline begged, "I'd rather stay. I'm really all right now."

She did not want to spoil Kathie's pleasure or drag Martin away so early. He had looked forward to this; it was his night.

The music had stopped, and Gustav Legrin was following Kathie across the floor to their table. Through the haze of introductions Arline was aware that Gavin was leaving the restaurant with his party. They passed behind her chair, and she could feel every muscle in her body grow tense as he drew level. Yet she knew he would not speak: she did not want him to speak.

The moment passed: she looked up to see his broad back disappearing through the glass doors in the wake of an elderly lady in grey.

Turning back to the table, she tried to force herself to be gay. Kathie and Gustav Legrin tossed the ball of conversation between them. For once Martin was silent. He seemed preoccupied with his drink, but every now and then Arline was aware of his brown eyes upon her with that look of concern still in their depths.

She heard Kathie invite Gustav Legrin to visit them at Fenmore House and see the advanced ballet class, and she knew that Legrin accepted with alacrity, but all that was going on about her seemed to be happening in another world, a remote world, in which she had no place. One fact alone dominated her mind. She had seen Gavin Shandon again, and that one brief glimpse of him told her more plainly than anything else could have done how much she still cared for him. She would never be able to forget him, not while there remained the possibility of meeting him, unawares at any odd moment of the day. One city was not big enough. Far better to cut completely adrift, to put distance between her and this ever-present danger of the wound in her heart being opened afresh.

Martin was at her elbow.

"I'm dropping Legrin at his hotel on the way home," he said. "Will you sit in front with me, Arline?"

Martin wanted her. Why not give him what happiness she could? She glanced at him in the sudden flashes of the street lamps. Companionship and understanding. Kathie had said they often counted for as much as love—afterwards. How long would it take her to forget Gavin in trying to make Martin happy?

The murmur of voices from the back seat came to her like the rise and fall of water, like the strange dark tide that heaved between two islands. The tide of circumstance.

If she went back to Canada with Martin there would be no hope of ever seeing Gavin again. Even that thought had power to hurt her. All the seas would roll between them. But it would be relief from this gnawing agony in her heart, the hope and the fear that some day, somewhere, she might see him again. Relief? Would she ever know relief—or forgetfulness?

They had stopped at an hotel in George Square and Legrin was saying good night. Kathie, more animated than she had ever appeared before, sat forward in her seat and talked of his ability all the way back to Charing Cross.

"Are you coming in, Martin?" she asked.

"No, not to-night, thanks," Martin replied, and Kathie did not press the point.

She stood on the top step and watched the red tail-light of her brother's car disappear into the mist of rain.

"Martin wasn't himself to-night," she said rather slowly, as she fumbled in her evening bag for the key.

Arline passed into the hall before her.

"Arline!"

Kathie had almost closed the heavy inner door when the voice broke in on the silence of the night. She turned sharply and peered out through the glass. A girl was standing in the porch, a wet tweed coat clutched round her slim form. Kathie opened the door wider, and in that instant Arline was past her.

"Helen! Helen, what are you doing here?"

"I came," Helen gasped. "I wanted to—to find you . . ."

She was almost fainting, and Arline led her quickly into the hall where Kathie had switched on the lights.

One glance at her cousin's pale face sent a stab of fear to Arline's heart. Helen was wet through, a fact which seemed to prove that she had been out in the rain for some considerable time. Swiftly she turned to her friend.

"It's my cousin—Helen—I've told you about her, Kathie. Can you help me to get her upstairs?"

Kathie was on Helen's other side in an instant, and between them they led her up to the flat.

"Get those wet things off her," Kathie directed, as she switched on the electric kettle which sat permanently by the side of the fire. "I'll get some brandy."

Arline was on her knees by Helen's side, rubbing her cold, wet hands between her own.

"Helen—Helen, dear, whatever made you stand about in all that rain? Why didn't you let me know you were coming? I would have stayed in."

A faint smile curved Helen's blue lips.

"I didn't know," she said. "I ran away."

The words came out in a rush, as if there was some relief in the telling of them.

"We'd better get her into your bed," Kathie said. "She's not in a fit state to go home to-night."

"I can't go home." Helen started up, something like panic in her voice. "Arline, I can't go back. Mother found out about Alex."

One short sentence—and how much it conveyed. Arline could vision all that Helen had been through. She turned to Kathie.

"Will you help her into my room? I'll 'phone to her people."

CHAPTER NINE

THE MIST HANGS LOW

I

DOWN in the hall, the well-remembered telephone number ready in her mind, Arline paused. What could she say to her aunt? Without doubt, Mrs. Penner would immediately accuse her of having had something to do with Helen's flight. Yet she knew that it was her duty to let her aunt know where Helen was. She lifted the receiver. After all, Helen might be able to rest better if she knew that there was no search being made for her.

"Hullo, Alice! This is Arline Hamilton speaking. Can you hear me?"

The maid's voice came, thin and reedy.

"Oh, miss—yes!"

"Is Mrs. Penner there, Alice?"

"She's just come in from the theatre, miss. She's gone up to her room. If you wait . . ."

The temptation was too much for Arline.

"Alice—just a minute—don't go."

"Yes, miss."

"Listen carefully, Alice. I want you to take a message to Mrs. Penner. Tell her—tell her that Miss Helen is spending the night with me. She came on a visit, and I think it is too wet for her to come home until the morning. Do you understand, Alice?"

"Yes—fine, miss."

"All right, Alice. Good-bye."

Arline rang off.

Little beads of perspiration were standing out on her upper lip, and she brushed her handkerchief across it as she ran back up the stairs to the flat.

Kathie was waiting for her in the lounge.

"Just a minute, Arline," she said, as Arline crossed towards the door of her own bedroom.

154

Something in the tone and the look on her friend's face pulled Arline up abruptly. She recrossed the lounge in half a dozen steps.

"Yes?"

"Arline, I don't like the look of Helen. No,"—swiftly—"I don't mean that I think she's ill—seriously ill—but she tells me she's been wandering about the streets for two hours in all that rain. She's fevered and shivering by turns, and, what worries me more, she doesn't even seem to have the energy to move now."

"I'll go in and see her," Arline said through dry lips.

Helen was lying on the bed in the shaded glow of the reading lamp. Her face was almost as white as the snowy linen, save for two unnaturally bright spots of colour high up on her cheeks and her hair was spread out on the pillow like gold thread tossed across it. Arline bent over her. The blue-veined eyelids looked almost transparent, and the suggestion of frailty was more marked than ever before. When the long lashes fluttered upwards at last, Helen's eyes were misted with pain. Her breath was coming through her dry lips like the fluttering of a bird's wing.

"Could I have the window open, Arline? It's so hard to —breathe."

Arline opened the window a little further, letting in a gust of rain-freshened air. There was a terrible fluttering thing at her own throat, and the tiny beads of perspiration had gathered on her lip again. Fear! She was afraid, as she realised she had been afraid for Helen in the past. She turned to find Kathie in the doorway looking across at the bed. The same thought was in both minds, but it was Kathie who voiced it first:

"We must get a doctor at once. I'll ring for Sibyll McCregan."

Arline sat dumbly by her cousin's bed until Dr. Sibyll McCregan's car pulled up in front of Fenmore House. She heard the bell peal, and Kathie going down to let the doctor in.

When Sibyll McCregan straightened and turned from the bed, her kindly green eyes took in Arline and Kathie in turn.

"There's nothing to be alarmed about at the moment," she said. "You did right in getting her to bed, though it was madness on her part to risk such a wetting in her condition."

She passed on into the lounge, and Arline followed her.

"You think she'll be all right?" she asked breathlessly.

"Yes, I think so." The doctor looked searchingly at Arline. "Is she some relation of yours? she asked.

"My cousin."

"What doctor is she under—her own doctor, I mean?" Sibyll McCregan asked, scribbling something on a scrap of paper.

"I don't think she was attending any doctor," Arline replied. "Of course, my aunt has a family doctor, but —I don't think Helen has seen him for some time."

The clutching fear was at her throat again. Something in the gravity of Sibyll McCregan's face seemed to hold her transfixed.

"I think you'd better get into touch with your aunt in the morning," she advised. "Your cousin needs special medical attention. She should have been having it years ago. It would be advisable to see her own doctor at once. She is suffering from a pulmonary disease, and each day wasted is a step in the wrong direction."

Long after the doctor had gone Arline stood where she had left her, holding on to the ridge of the low mantelpiece as if, without its support, she must collapse. Kathie found her there when she returned from the hall.

"Sit down, Arline," she said, guiding her friend towards the divan. "Let me make you a cup of tea."

"I—couldn't drink it, Kathie."

Arline felt as if a bleak wind was sweeping over her. Helen! Helen! Her cousin's name rose from her heart like the cry of some wounded creature in a lone, waste place. Helen—so young—so beautiful!

Kathie knelt on the divan and put her arms round her friend's shoulders.

"Don't fret, Arline. We must look after Helen," she said, "and you can't do that if you let yourself go to pieces."

The need for some kind of service pulled Arline together as nothing else could have done. She rose to her feet and helped Kathie to fill hot water bottles and tuck them in at Helen's feet to ward off the chill that might so easily prove fatal. She was working now with the calmness which necessity brings, her own heartache forgotten in this greater need, and not until Helen had dozed off into a natural sleep, her breathing almost normal again, did she permit herself to relax.

"You'll have that cup of tea now," Kathie said, "and then you must get some sleep yourself."

It was after two o'clock, but Kathie insisted on making the proffered cup of tea, and as Arline sat drinking it some of the numbness seemed to go out of her.

"Kathie," she said at last, laying down her empty cup, "I must go and see my aunt to-morrow morning."

Kathie glanced at her quickly.

"But I thought she made things rather hot for you while you lived there?" she said.

"I know." Arline's eyes were fixed on the dying embers of the fire. "But someone has to tell her about Helen."

"Couldn't you 'phone?"

Arline shook her head.

"It's not the sort of thing that one can telephone," she said huskily. "I must go. I must see Aunt Hilda myself."

"I understand," Kathie replied quietly.

She knew that no matter what had transpired in the past, no grudge would keep her friend from doing what she could for Helen, and when Arline rose early the next morning and came back into the bedroom half an hour later with a breakfast tray in her hands, Kathie said:

"You shouldn't have bothered about my breakfast. I must get up and look after Helen while you are away."

"She looks all right this morning," Arline said, with a faint smile. "There's no sign of chill, and she was sleeping soundly when I went in."

"All the same," Kathie replied, "we'll just keep her in bed to-day."

"I won't be gone very long," Arline said, slipping into her coat."

It was early to make a call, and she knew that her aunt might not be up yet, but as she turned into Westwood Drive, Arline was quite prepared to wait any length of time to see Mrs. Penner.

Alice opened the door in answer to her ring.

"Oh, miss—come in!"

Arline stepped into the familiar hall with its expanse of red Turkish carpet and wide staircase leading to the corridors of the first floor.

Stupid to be waiting like a stranger in a house where you had lived for years, she thought. Alice came back, her smile apologetic.

"Mrs. Penner can't see anyone, miss," she said. "She's not too well this morning."

The old alibi; the old pose—and the tragedy back there at Fenmore House! Arline was past the maid and at the dining-room door.

"I must see her, Alice," she said firmly. "I'll take the responsibility of this—intrusion."

She knocked at the door and went in.

Mrs. Penner was seated at the dining-table alone, the remains of her late breakfast before her. She was spreading marmalade on a finger of buttered toast, but her knife fell to the plate when she looked up and saw the intruder.

"I told Alice distinctly . . ." she began, but something in the look on Arline's face silenced her.

"Aunt Hilda, I must speak to you. I haven't come here for any reason of my own. It's about Helen."

"About encouraging her to stay away from home, do you mean?" Mrs. Penner's tone was dry.

Suddenly Arline felt overwhelmingly sorry for her aunt. That strange woman sitting there proudly in her costly *négligé* in the over-decorated room, her face already made-up like a mask, her hard blue eyes full of animosity, could not guess the blow that was about to be dealt her. A deep note of compassion crept into Arline's voice.

"I didn't encourage Helen, Aunt Hilda, but that is beside the point now," she said. "She came to look for me last night. I was out, and she waited about in the rain." She paused, waiting for some sign of anxiety from the woman across the table. "Aunt Hilda, have you no idea that Helen is ill—very ill? She's been ill for months, perhaps years."

"What are you saying?"

There was a faint note of concern in Mrs. Penner's voice at last. She even rose from her seat at the foot of the table.

"Helen's seriously ill," Arline went on quickly. "We had to send for a doctor last night and—and she said that Helen must be given treatment at once. You must take her to your own doctor right away. She's never been strong, Aunt Hilda. Oh! can't you see . . ."

Mrs. Penner came round the end of the table and gripped Arline's arm.

"What are you trying to tell me?" She recoiled before the truth in her niece's eyes. "No—oh, God! Not that! That can't happen to me—to Helen!"

There was mingled horror and dismay in her voice now, and she seemed incapable of thought or action. It was left to Arline to suggest and advise.

"Let me ring for Dr. Burchall," she said kindly. "You'll feel better when you've had his advice."

Mrs. Penner seemed willing to let her do anything, and when Arline had given Dr. Burchall the address of Fenmore House over the telephone, her aunt went upstairs and was down in the hall again dressed for the street in less than ten minutes.

Coats brought round the car, and they were in Charing Cross in a quarter of an hour. Dr. Burchall had arrived before them, and Kathie came out of the bedroom as Mrs. Penner went in.

"Helen seems all right again this morning," she said to Arline. "Perhaps—do you think it possible that Sibyll McCregan could have made a mistake last night?"

But Sibyll McCregan had made no mistake. Dr. Burchall confirmed her diagnosis. He sat in the lounge alone with Mrs. Penner for a very long time after they had left Helen's bedside. An hour later Kathie went downstairs to show him out.

Mrs. Penner rose from the divan. Her shoulders were bowed a little, and her eyes were like those of an old pain-burdened woman in the mask of her carefully massaged face.

"I've arranged to take Helen to Switzerland," she said in a low voice. "There's just the chance that the air there may save the other lung. If she can stay here until to-morrow, I will be grateful to your friend. It may be unwise to move her to-day."

"Aunt Hilda—oh, Aunt Hilda, I'm sorry," Arline cried from her full heart, but Mrs. Penner scarcely seemed to hear her.

She went downstairs and out to her car like a woman in a dream.

The following morning the Daimler called again at Fenmore House. Coats carried up a fur wrap for Helen and a basket of fruit and a box of flowers addressed to Arline and Kathie.

Helen put the wrap on automatically. The old look of resignation was in her eyes again as she kissed her cousin good-bye.

"I'm going to Switzerland," she said quietly. "At least there will be sunshine there."

II

"And now that I have taught you all I know about Canadian cookery," Martin said, surveying the lemon pie that lay, gold and steaming, on the wire tray on the kitchen table, "what answer are you going to give me to the perpetual question?"

Arline folded her cooking apron and laid it in the drawer. The smile had faded from her lips, and when she looked across at Martin her eyes were troubled.

"Need I answer just yet?" she asked, conscious, even as she did so, of the uselessness of playing for time. Something told her that Martin's perseverence would win in the end.

He came over to where she stood and put a friendly arm about her shoulders.

"I can't put off that sailing date much longer," he reminded her with one of his affectionate smiles. "I know I'm not the big passion, but that would come, Arline."

Would it? Would it? Her heart was hammering in her breast. She thought that she had made up her mind that night on the way home from the Q Restaurant when the one brief glimpse of Gavin had shown her how hopeless forgetfullness would be while she still remained in Glasgow. She *had* made up her mind, but now the words which Martin declared would make him the happiest man in the world seemed to stick in her throat. She could not give him her promise—yet. But she knew that Martin could not wait for ever. Although he had a competent foreman in charge of the ranch, he had told her that he must be back in Canada before the end of the year.

Why not answer now? Why not tell Martin that she was willing to go with him—become his wife?

She turned towards him, and at that moment Kathie came through the swing doors and glanced from one to the other.

"What's going on here?" she demanded laughingly. "Don't you realise I have a class in ten minutes time, and a visitor to tea?"

"Legrin isn't our responsibility," her brother reminded her airily. "What's he coming for, anyway?"

Kathie was giving all her attention to her examination of the lemon pie.

"To see the ballet class, of course," she replied without looking up.

"Don't you mean the ballet-mistress?" Martin asked, and ducked his head quickly to avoid the wooden spoon his sister was childish enough to aim at him. "All right," he laughed from a safer distance. "We understand! Stranger things have been done in the name of love."

"Martin, don't be disgusting," Kathie cried. "Gus—Mr. Legrin is coming to see my class, and I have hopes that he might find someone worth taking up."

Arline was immediately interested by the latter part of Kathie's statement.

"Do you think he might notice Sheena McCallum-Blair?" she asked.

"I think he might," Kathie said. "Anyway, I'll give her all the limelight I can without making it too obvious."

"She deserves a chance," Arline said, moving towards the door. "She's awfully keen."

"And you seem keen enough to see her succeed," Kathie smiled.

Visitors often sat on the piano platform to watch Kathie's ballet pupils at practice, but it seemed that afternoon that Sheena McCallum-Blair was aware of Gustav Legrin's identity from the moment he sat down just a little behind Arline and prepared to watch. Sheena danced as she had never danced before. She seemed inspired, and she was like thistledown on her toes. There was no trace of nervousness, no self-consciousness; she was a born dancer. At the end of an hour Arline began to convince herself that Gustave Legrin was impressed.

"Well, what do you think of them?" Kathie asked eagerly.

"A clever display, Kay, and very much worth while watching. I congratulate you," her visitor smiled.

Arline was as disappointed as if she had been Sheena McCallum-Blair. Couldn't Legrin see that the girl was good, she thought, as she followed Martin upstairs.

During the meal the conversation turned to Canada and little was said about dancing. Kathie sat rather dreamily in a corner of the big divan, her small feet tucked under her, and watched Legrin without saying very much. Arline wondered if her friend was as disappointed as she felt herself. She knew that Kathie had been eager for recognition for Sheena McCallum-Blair, and that she had coached the girl more carefully than any other pupil.

When Legrin rose to leave, Kathie went with him to the front door.

"How long has Kathie known Legrin?" Arline asked.

Martin considered.

"She's known him for about three years," he said, "and worshipped from afar for about six or seven, I think."

"She met him in London, didn't she?"

"Yes—when she was down studying for her letters."

"He's much older than she is."

"About ten years," Martin said. "What's that in a lifetime?"

"Nothing," Arline replied, "if she cares for him."

Martin looked across at her quickly.

"What exactly do you demand of love, Arline?" he asked, after a moment's consideration.

"I don't know." She moved restlessly in her chair, and because the question troubled her she turned it on him. "What do you demand, Martin?"

He looked at her with a smile in his eyes.

"I thought you knew that," he said.

He came across to her and sat down on the arm of her chair.

"Well, I'll tell you again," he said. "Love to me is the meeting of two people who understand each other

162

thoroughly, who have the same tastes, the same outlook on life, and who are prepared to give and take—fifty-fifty in everything."

"Isn't that—friendship?"

"Friendship between men," he said. "It could be love between a man and a woman."

"Isn't there—something more?"

"Yes"—slowly—"I believe there is. That undefinable something that even I can't put a name to."

"And if it's missing, Martin, that undefinable something?"

He laughed.

"Are you trying to tell me again that I'm wasting my time?"

Arline got to her feet.

"No, no! I am trying to tell you that I can't offer you second best," she cried. "I've felt that—that undefinable something before, Martin, and—oh, can't you see, it can never be the same again! It just wouldn't be fair."

"To whom?"

"To you," Arline's eyes were moist with emotion. "I've nothing to offer you."

Martin crossed the short space between them.

"And if I tell you that what you have to give is enough?" he asked. "Would that make a difference?"

"I don't know. It hardly seems fair."

"Fair or not, I want you. I've guessed there was once someone else in your life, and I was rotten enough to pump Kathie about the affair. I know what I'm asking for, Arline, and I'm asking you again." He took her hand, looking directly into her troubled eyes. "When will you give me my answer?"

"Before you sail," she promised, and Martin was content with that.

III

Three weeks after Helen's departure for Switzerland, Alex Framer called at Fenmore House and asked to see Arline. She was alone that afternoon; there were no classes, so Kathie had taken the opportunity of going to a *matinée* with Gustav Legrin, and Arline had settled down to clear up some arrears of secretarial work.

Waiting for Alex to be shown up to her office, she wondered what he would be like, but she was scarcely prepared for the fair-haired boy who was shown into the room. He reminded her instantly of Douglas, with his incredibly blue eyes and sunburned skin, but there were lines about his mouth that were ageing when she looked at him a second time.

"My name's Framer—Alex Framer," he introduced himself. "Helen has told you about me?"

The words were scarcely a question, yet Arline treated them as such.

"Yes, she told me." She held out her hand. "I've wanted to meet you for a long time, Alex."

He shook hands almost eagerly.

"I've been looking forward to meeting you," he said gravely, and then the blue eyes darkened as a shadow passed in them. "I'm going out to her," he ended slowly.

"To Switzerland?"

He nodded.

"Yes. Mrs. Penner sent for me. I work for an uncle, and he is quite willing to give me the time off, provided I'm back before the Christmas rush begins in the shop."

"Helen's not—worse?" Arline asked, anxiety in every line of her face.

"No. She wanted to see me, that's all."

"And—my aunt sent for you?"

He nodded again, scarcely seeming to notice the incredulity in her voice.

"I thought I'd like to meet you before I went out," he continued. "Helen always spoke so much about you, and she gave me your address. Perhaps you'd like to send a message?"

Arline's eyes misted over with tears, and she looked down at the desk before her.

"Yes," she whispered at last, "tell her—tell her that I know everything is going to be all right now."

"Thank you." Framer rose to his feet. "I won't keep you any longer, for I know you are busy, and I have only a few minutes of my lunch hour left. I felt that I had to see you, Miss Hamilton. I hope you don't mind me coming?"

"I'm glad you came," Arline told him. "Will you call again and tell me how Helen is when you come back from Switzerland?"

"I will," he said. "Thank you."

There was no need to wonder if Alex Framer cared for Helen as deeply as she cared for him. It was in every line of his face, in the changed tone of his voice when he spoke her name.

Kathie must have passed him on her way out to meet Legrin, for when she arrived back at Fenmore House just in time for tea she asked immediately:

"Who was the fair giant you had to visit you as I went out? He asked me in rather awed tones where he might find Miss Hamilton."

"Alex Framer," Arline replied. "The boy Helen was so keen on."

Kathie halted on her way to the bedroom.

"There's nothing wrong?"

Arline shook her head.

"No. He's going out to see Helen, and he called to ask if I'd like to send her a message. Kathie, Aunt Hilda actually sent for him."

"I thought this trouble might change that woman," Kathie said. "It generally takes something like that to make selfish people aware of themselves. She hasn't written to you yet?"

"Whom? Helen?"

"No—your aunt."

"I don't expect her to. She hasn't done me an injustice— not to the extent that she did Helen and Alex."

"Are you quite sure?" Kathie asked.

"What do you mean?"

"Oh, nothing. Just an idea I had." Kathie tossed her hat through the open door of her bedroom, smiling with satisfaction when it landed safely on the bed. "I've got some good news for you."

"Oh. What?"

"Gus Legrin *did* notice Sheena. He wants to take her back to London with him when he goes. He says she's got the stuff in her that, with careful handling, will make her an international success."

"Oh, how marvellous!" Arline cried. "Why didn't he say so before? I thought he wasn't impressed."

"So did I, but seemingly he's like that," Kathie declared. "He thinks things over from every angle before he'll commit himself."

"She'll be delighted," Arline smiled. "I can just see her face when you tell her."

Kathie began to set out the cups for tea.

"I don't want to tell Sheena yet," she said. "I don't want to disappoint the child by building her hopes up before I have seen her parents."

"Of course," Arline agreed slowly. "You'll have to get Mrs. McCallum-Blair's permission."

"Yes, I must go and see her some time soon. Gus will let me have all the particulars in a day or two." Kathie gazed into the fire. "He's thinking of starting his own ballet school in London."

"How nice! Does he want Sheena to attend it?"

"Yes." Kathie seemed scarcely conscious of having made the reply. "He's asked me to join it, too," she said, at last.

"To join it?" Arline echoed.

"Yes, in a rather unusual capacity. He wants me to go into partnership."

"In the school? Oh, how fine!" Arline was genuinely glad for her friend.

"In more than the school," Kathie replied. "In—a home, too."

"Oh, Kathie! You're going to marry him?"

"I haven't given him my answer yet. It's a big step, you know," Kathie replied.

"But you *do* care for him?"

"Yes, I care for him."

"Then . . . You're not thinking of your work?" Arline asked.

"I was," Kathie admitted. "It means a lot to me."

"Yes, I know," Arline replied, "but—doesn't love mean more?"

Kathie rose.

"I'm trying to convince myself that it doesn't, but I am beginning to have a feeling that the little blind god will win in the end." She was smiling as she stood looking down into the glowing heart of the coals. "Love versus career—the old, old question!"

"If you're going into partnership with Mr. Legrin, you'd still have your career," Arline reminded her.

"It won't be the same," Kathie said. "I wonder if I can make you understand? This place is *mine*. I built it up alone. It's part of my very blood—I've lived for it." She turned away and walked the length of the room and back again. "Perhaps it's foolish of me to be talking like this, but it's how I feel. You should be interested too, you know."

"I am, Kathie," Arline replied, "but I think you would make a great mistake if you refused Mr. Legrin—caring for him, I mean."

Kathie paused in her restless pacing.

"You don't think about yourself much, Arline do you?" she said.

"In what way?"

"Well, if I go to London you'd be out of a job."

That thought had passed through Arline's mind at the beginning of the conversation, but she had dismissed it.

"I'd have to find something else to do," she said lightly, but when Kathie had passed on into the bedroom the thought recurred.

The prospect of being unemployed again was not exactly a rosy one, yet she considered it, weighing it in the balance against the prospect of becoming Martin Lang's wife. She knew that she could never feel the supreme passion for Martin, but there would be friendship and mutual interest, and a complete understanding between them. Was that not compensation enough for love? Why not? Love had spelt disillusionment and heartache for her, and now she was faced by the prospect of being alone again. Perhaps that was what frightened her most. Kathie would marry Gustav Legrin and Martin would go back to Canada. All that she had built up here in friendship around her would be gone. She would have nobody—nothing but memories. It seemed that fate was spurring her on, more surely and steadily as each day passed, to give Martin the answer he desired.

It was a full week, however, before Kathie made up her mind, and when she told Arline that morning at breakfast her voice was almost apologetic.

"I'm going to marry Gus," she said, "just as soon as we can get everything arranged."

"I'm glad," Arline replied simply. "I thought you would see things that way in the end, Kathie."

"Of course, I must continue here until the end of the present quarter and send out notices to my pupils," Kathie continued. "We'll have a lot to do, Arline, between now and Christmas, and it's only a few weeks."

"I won't mind being kept busy," Arline assured her.

To be kept too busy to think was her salvation these days, and she welcomed this prospect of more work so that she might not have too much time to dwell upon her own problems.

"I must find time to see Sheena McCallum-Blair's parents soon," Kathie went on. "Would you write to the mother and ask if I might have an appointment some time? I'll tell you when Gus gets everything fixed up."

"Yes," Arline said, almost inaudibly.

The bell pealed down in the hall, and Kathie rose from the table.

"That will be the post," she said.

Arline turned to take it when Milly brought it up.

"Any personals?" Kathie asked.

Arline ran through the small bundle of letters.

"Just one for me," she said slowly, "from Switzerland."

"From Helen?" Kathie asked, interested at once.

Arline slit the flap of the envelope.

"I don't recognise the handwriting," she said, extracting the sheet of notepaper.

Her eyes travelled across the closely-written page, and gradually every vestige of colour drained from her face. She sat down suddenly in the chair she had vacated and stared before her with unseeing eyes. Kathie crossed to her side.

"Arline—what is it?"

"It's Helen. She's dead."

The whispered words seemed to paralyse Kathie; she stood still, gazing down at the white, fluttering sheet of paper in her friend's hand as if she could not believe they had been uttered. Arline handed the letter to her.

"It's from Alex. He got there just in time." She rose to her feet and crossed to the window where a shaft of wintry sunshine had strayed into the room. When she spoke again her voice was so low that Kathie wondered if she had addressed her at all. "She would be happy," she said huskily. "She always knew they would be—together in the end."

CHAPTER TEN

THE OLIVE BRANCH

I

MRS. PENNER sat before the fire in the long drawing-room at Westwood Drive and fumbled with the handkerchief which lay in the lap of her severe black dress. She glanced from time to time at the gold face of the little clock ticking the minutes away under its glass dome on the mantelpiece. She had sent for Arline, and she wondered if the girl would come. Her ears were strained for each sound on the gravel of the drive, and when the door-bell rang at last she rose and crossed to the window. She was standing there when Arline was shown in.

"You sent for me, Aunt Hilda," Arline said, her voice shaking a little in spite of her brave determination to remain composed.

She had written to her aunt on Helen's death, and had not received a reply until the short note which had been delivered the day before at Fenmore House asking her to come to Westwood Drive.

"Sit down, won't you?" Mrs. Penner indicated a chair which had been pulled up close to the fire. "I'll ring for some tea. It's very cold outside."

She turned to press the bell, and the light from the big bay window fell full upon her face. It had little lines of suffering on it, and for the first time for years massage and uplift had been forgotten. The stamp of sorrow had erased the cold blue look from her eyes, and they were almost kind.

When the tea had been served, and they were alone again, she said:

"I sent for you because I want you to come back here, Arline." She paused, but as Arline made no reply she went on again slowly. "I know I—I treated you badly in the past, but all that can be put right now. I want you to make your home with us again, if you will?"

Arline knew just how difficult it must have been for a woman like her aunt to have made that speech, and she felt sorry for Mrs. Penner from the bottom of her heart. Yet she felt that she could not bring herself to comply with her aunt's wishes.

"I'm very happy in the work I'm doing, Aunt Hilda," she pointed out.

"You would not need to work here," Mrs. Penner said. "Everything would be different."

Arline knew that remorse was driving her to make this offer.

"It's kind of you," she said gratefully, "but I don't think I could." She saw the blank look of disappointment which spread across her aunt's face, and decided that she could only handle the situation by being perfectly frank. "It's not coming back here that really matters," she continued slowly, "but, Aunt Hilda, you will see my point when I tell you that I couldn't bear to meet the McCallum-Blairs—as I must surely do if I stayed here."

The truth of her refusal sent the painful colour of deep embarrassment flooding into Mrs. Penner's cheeks.

"That was another thing in which I had no right to interfere," she said with difficulty.

"To interfere?" A strange and rather pitiful little smile touched Arline's lips. "You only told me the truth I couldn't see for myself."

There was a deep silence, and then Mrs. Penner's voice breaking in upon it almost harshly:

"I didn't tell you the truth."

Arline looked up.

"What do you mean?"

"I told you the truth as far as it suited myself." Mrs. Penner seemed determined to humble herself by the whole appalling truth now. "There *was* a certain amount of gossip at Glen Solan, but not nearly as much as I led you to believe. Mrs. McCallum-Blair never heard it."

Arline jumped to her feet, her breath coming swiftly between her parted lips.

"You mean—Gavin didn't really just propose out of—out of pity?"

Mrs. Penner bowed her head.

"As far as I know, he didn't."

171

"Then—you made it up? You told me that for—for . . ."

Arline was choking with suppressed emotion. She clenched her hands at her side, for at the moment she felt that she could have struck the woman before her. And then the futility of anger presented itself. What good would it do? Confessions and sorrow and truth. What use were they all now? She had lost Gavin anyway, and *that* dreadful truth only made it harder to bear.

"I don't suppose you could ever bring yourself to forgive me?"

It seemed a pitiful thing for her aunt to be asking her forgiveness. She remembered the Mrs. Penner of former scenes, and thought her aunt did not seem the same woman.

"I don't know whether forgiveness can make such a lot of difference," she said, "but—for Helen's sake— we'll say no more about it." She turned and picked up her gloves and bag from the table just inside the door. "I'm sorry I can't come back, Aunt Hilda, but I don't feel as if I possibly could."

Mrs. Penner was looking at her as if she could not believe that she had actually refused.

"If you ever change your mind," she said, "you'll let me know?"

"Yes, if I ever change my mind," Arline agreed.

She was out in the street at last, bewildered, unhappy. What a mess. What a stupid, unnecessary blunder! And yet the fact remained that Gavin had cared for some-one else. Could that have been another fabrication of her aunt's? But Mrs. Penner had brought back that information the day she had gone to visit Mrs. McCallum-Blair at Rowan Gate. She did not pause to think that Mrs. Penner had brought back the other information ostensibly from Rowan Gate that same day and had just now confessed that it was not the truth, nor did it occur to her that Mrs. McCallum-Blair might have been too ill that afternoon to receive callers or gossip with them.

When she reached Fenmore House, Kathie was just dismissing a class, and she came out of the ball-room as Arline entered the hall. One glance at her friend's face told her that something was wrong, but she felt that Arline would confide in her in her own time.

"Have you had tea?" she asked, slipping her arm through her friend's as they went upstairs together.

"Yes," Arline answered dully. "Aunt Hilda gave me some."

"What did she want?" Kathie asked, kicking off her dancing shoes in favour of a pair of comfortable slippers.

"She wanted me to go back there."

"As unpaid secretary?"

"No. She offered me a home."

"Oh?" Kathie glanced doubtfully at her friend. "Are you going to accept?"

Arline shook her head.

"I couldn't," she said. "Kathie—she told me that— that she had interfered in—in my affair with Gavin. She confessed that most of what she told me before was untrue."

Kathie stood for a moment without speaking. Then:

"What are you going to do?" she asked.

"Nothing," Arline replied flatly. "What can I do?"

"Why don't you go to Shandon and tell him the truth?"

"I can't—now."

Arline's tone seemed to lack interest, and Kathie confessed inwardly that she did not know what to think. The whole thing was a gigantic muddle from beginning to end, and she felt that she wanted to shake somebody—Arline not excluded.

Gustav Legrin was expected to tea, and Milly showed him up to the lounge almost on their heels. He greeted them both in his quiet way, bending down to kiss Kathie on the cheek.

Arline knew that her friend was looking directly at her but she did not look up. She knew what Kathie was thinking, and the fact that Martin's departure was only ten days away brought her own thoughts round to the promise she had made. Her aunt's confession could make little difference, she told herself, and to see Gavin married to someone else was more than she could bear. She made up her mind. She would tell Martin to-night—give him the answer he wanted.

173

Now that her mind was finally made up she accepted the decision with almost fatalistic calm. It was the way things worked out.

"Have you interviewed that young lady's mother yet?" Gustav Legrin asked Kathie, accepting his tea-cup from her.

"No," she replied, "I was waiting until we had all the details ready to put before her, but if you're all fixed up now Arline can write to Mrs. McCallum-Blair in the morning. I should be able to see her some time this week."

"I don't think there's anything else to wait for," Legrin said. "You can give her the address of the school now, and she can make enquiries—look up my character, so to speak."

Kathie laughed.

"Do you think you could remember that in the morning, Arline?" she asked. "They live in Bearsden somewhere, but you'll get the address from the ledger."

Arline, who knew the address only too well, said she would attend to the matter first thing in the morning, and went through to her own bedroom to change.

Kathie and Legrin were going on to a theatre after dinner in the Q Restaurant, and Arline knew that Martin would be coming round shortly to take her out. He would no doubt suggest a quiet little supper somewhere. She could give him her answer in the restaurant, she thought. What did the place matter? And then the vision of Puck's Glen rose before her, and a man's deep voice sounded in her ears: "Arline, haven't you guessed it, my dear? I love you." She pressed the back of her hand against her quivering mouth while the scalding tears gathered in her eyes and coursed down her cheeks unheeded. How could he have said that and not meant it?"

She dressed slowly, with an empty feeling in her heart that she knew was quite wrong for someone who was about to tell a man she would marry him. But, after all, Martin knew. He would not expect too much.

She tried not to think of the interview at Westwood Drive and her aunt's confession, but her mind kept reverting to the one question. What would have happened if Mrs. Penner had not interfered?

Yet, she thought, it was little use to ask herself that now. The past was dead. Why rake over the grey ashes? Surely somewhere there was a spark that would kindle another fire. The steady, glowing fire of friendship with Martin. . . .

Feeling that she wanted to be alone as long as possible, she sat in her room until she heard Martin's voice in the lounge. When she went in Kathie was pouring her brother a cocktail.

"These two are deserting us to-night, Arline," he said with mock disgust. "They're sneaking off to the theatre on their own."

"You know you refused to come," Kathie reminded him. "You said the ballet was too highbrow for you."

"It is. I confess my low tastes are all for a variety show," Martin laughed. "But perhaps Arline would have liked to go?"

"I don't really mind," Arline said. "I can see the ballet another time."

"That doesn't sound very hopeful for me," Martin remarked, as they went out together. "The ballet never gets as far West as Crystal Falls."

She could have told him now, Arline thought, promised to go back to the ranch at Crystal Falls with him, but the words stuck in her throat. Her final promise refused to shape itself in words. Later—later! There's time enough. There's the whole evening to tell him in. The persistent little voice within her won.

"Where would you like to go?" Martin asked, opening the door of the car for her to get in. "A movie?"

"Yes, if you like."

He stood with his foot on the running board and looked up at the night sky.

"It's a grand night," he said, with that appreciation of wide open spaces which was yet another thing they had in common. "To grand to sit in a hall looking at a movie. And I believe there's going to be a moon. Are you wrapped up well enough to go for a spin?"

"Yes, I'm warm enough," Arline replied.

"Then—is it settled?"

"Yes."

She sat back in the car as it moved away. That terrible feeling of unreality was gripping her again. It seemed that someone else was acting for her. She sat still and upright in her seat while the car gathered speed outside the town. Quite unconscious of direction, she left the choice of their destination to Martin. She knew that he could not fail to notice her listlessness, but she felt that it was better than a forced animation that could deceive neither of them. They were out on the Fenwick moors before she took any notice of their surroundings.

It was a clear, starry night, with frost sharp and keen in the air, and a crescent moon just appearing over the edge of the hills. The whole firmament seemed alive with stars, twinkling down to the very edge of the earth. On any other night she would have gloried in the breathtaking beauty of it all, but to-night her thoughts could only dwell on one subject, although she could not bring herself to voice them.

Martin had pressed his foot down on the accelerator, and they were flying along with the ease and speed of a bird. The car was pleasing him to-night after its overhaul, and, as he slowed down to take the turn from the moors on to the main road, he smiled to himself. Then, as if it had been wiped from his face, the smile gave place to a look of mingled horror and dismay.

"My God! the fellow's on his wrong side!"

A big saloon was bearing down upon them, swinging well out as it turned the bend. With almost superhuman strength Martin swung his car round and up on the grass verge at the side of the road. There was a sickening moment of suspense before it turned over and rolled to the bottom of the bank.

The saloon had held the road, and the man at the wheel, pale and rather shaken now, got out and came across to where Martin was easing himself out of the driving seat.

"Let me lend you a hand, old man," he said. "Do you think you're hurt?"

"Never mind about me," Martin said between clenched teeth.

He was almost blind with rage at the other's folly, but his first thought was for Arline.

"Turn your headlights on here," he commanded, and when the man had done his bidding rather sheepishly, he found Arline where she had been thrown when the car took that first wild leap into the air.

She was lying so deathly still that for a moment he thought she was past all human aid, and his limbs almost refused to carry him to the spot. At last he reached her, bending down swiftly to pillow her head on his arm. A faint moan escaped her lips as he moved her.

"Arline . . .!"

He could not—he dare not move her farther. He tried to loosen the fur collar round her throat, cursing inwardly at the inefficiency of his trembling fingers.

"My brother's gone to 'phone for help," the man from the other car said, but Martin scarcely seemed to hear.

Not until a doctor arrived on the scene ten minutes later did he pause in his efforts to bring Arline back to consciousness.

II

The telephone bell hummed as Kathie Lang opened the glass door and stepped into the hall.

"Who can that be at this time of night?" she said, lifting the instrument while she smiled at Gustav Legrin over it.

"Perhaps Martin's stuck somewhere," her companion suggested. "I hope we don't have to go and tow him in."

He took an idle turn around the hall and came back to the table. At sight of his fiancée's changed face, he asked quickly:

"What's the matter, Kay?"

Kathie was listening intently, her eyes full of horror, and murmuring a low "yes" from time to time to the speaker at the other end of the line. When she replaced the instrument on its stand at last, she turned quickly to Legrin.

"Gus, can you get me a taxi?" she said. "It was Martin. He's had an accident with the car and—Arline's hurt. They've taken her to Highmoor hospital. I must get there at once."

Legrin looked down at the thin theatre coat she was wearing.

"I'll 'phone for a taxi," he said. "You run upstairs and get a warmer coat. The taxi can't be here for five minutes or so, and you'll have plenty of time."

She obeyed him automatically, picking a fur coat at random from her wardrobe and changing her low-cut sandals for a pair of shoes. When she came down to the hall again the taxi was drawing up at the front door.

Legrin gave the instructions.

"Take us to Highmoor hospital as quickly as you can," he said. "How did it happen?" he asked, as the car moved away.

"Some fool on the road—speeding, I suppose," Kathie replied. "Martin didn't say much. He was too concerned about Arline. Oh, Gus—if anything should happen to her. . . ."

He put his arm protectingly round her.

"Don't worry yet, Kay," he said gently. "We're getting to her as quickly as we can."

Minutes seemed hours to Kathie on that journey across the moors with the great stars looking down out of the frosty sky like a million watching eyes.

"Will we never come to it?" she said to Legrin, and, as if in answer to her frenzied question, the taxi swung to the left and took the narrow road to Highmoor.

The big, many-gabled building stood out against the night sky with only one light burning in an upstairs window. When they rang the bell a porter appeared at the door and, with maddening deliberation, escorted them up the broad flight of stairs to the first floor.

"Wait here," he commanded, and disappeared through a swing door.

Kathie felt for Legrin's hand, holding on to it silently. Minutes passed. It seemed that the quiet of the place was a tangible thing that almost touched them.

The door opened at last, and the porter came out, followed by Martin. Kathie saw her brother's white face through a sudden mist of tears.

"Martin . . .!"

"Come in here," he said, leading them through the swing door to a room which opened on the left.

"How is she, Martin?" Kathie's voice was shaking with anxiety.

"Pretty bad, I think. I've only seen her once since we brought her in. Concussion, the doctors say." His voice sank to a low murmur. "She's unconscious again."

A deep silence descended on the room. Neither Legrin nor Kathie seemed inclined to break it. At last Martin said:

"Kathie, who's this fellow Shandon—Gavin Shandon?"

Kathie started up.

"Gavin Shandon," she repeated, her eyes blank for a moment. "Oh, he's the man Arline was to have married."

"I thought so." Martin took a quick, uneasy turn round the room as if he were finding difficulty in making a decision. "Where can we find him?" he asked, at last.

There was a moment's pause, and then Kathie said heavily:

"I don't know."

Martin sat down on the chair next to hers, leaning his arms on the table.

"Don't think you're helping me by holding back the truth, Kathie," he said steadily. "If you know you must tell me. Arline's been calling for him incessantly ever since we brought her here."

"Martin, I don't know. Do you think I'd lie to you at a time like this? Arline gave me the barest details when—when she told me about him."

Kathie's even white teeth bit into her lower lip. It had not taken this crisis to make her aware that Arline was still deeply in love with the man who had saved her life at Glen Solan. She had sensed it for a very long time, and her heart had been afraid for her brother.

But this changed everything. Gavin Shandon must be found—wherever he was.

"Do you think I may see her?" she asked.

"I don't know. I'll ask the night sister."

Martin went out with that quick, stealthy tread which he seemed to have acquired during the past few hours in the hospital. Kathie sat on at the table, staring at the highly polished surface and seeing mirrored there a

179

hundred possible ways in which the accident had happened.

"Is there no hope of tracing this fellow Shandon?" Legrin asked, sitting down by her side.

"I don't know. Somehow I can't just think—clearly—yet." Kathie said. "There must be some way, of course. . . ."

Martin came round the door.

"You can see her for a moment, Kathie—but only a moment. The nurse will take you up."

He opened the door for her, and when the nurse had led her away along the corridor he came back into the room and sat down beside Legrin.

"My God! this suspense," he said between his teeth, "and the doctors asking me to find this fellow Shandon!"

"Surely there's some way of getting into touch with him?" Legrin asked. "Buck up, man! Kathie will find him if he's to be found anywhere. Give her a minute or two to collect her thoughts. She's had a bit of a shock, too, you know."

"Yes, I know," Martin said. "I wish to heaven we had stayed in town with you."

The door opened and Kathie came slowly into the room.

"I'm going back to the flat," she said. "I must see if I can find anything among Arline's papers that will help me to trace Gavin Shandon. You'll stay here, I suppose, Martin?"

"For a while yet. She may regain consciousness again and want someone she knows near her."

The drive back to town seemed endless, and Kathie, sitting upright and silent in the jolting taxi, was thankful beyond measure for Legrin's presence and the wordless understanding of his protective arm round her shoulders.

When Arline's few belongings yielded no trace of Shandon's address, she sat down on the edge of her friend's office desk and stared unseeingly at the spent ashes in the big, open grate.

"We can't do anything else until the morning," she said to Legrin, who had sat silently watching as she made her search. "Then I must 'phone her aunt and ask her for Shandon's address."

"And meanwhile," Legrin said, rising and coming over to where she sat, "I suppose your own work has to go on to-morrow?" He took out his watch and looked at it. "It's almost three o'clock, Kay. I want you to promise me that you'll go to bed and get some sleep the moment I leave."

"I promise," she said, rising and laying her head against his rough tweed coat with a little weary gesture. "I'll connect the telephone through to my bedroom in case there is a call from Martin."

She knew that she was keyed up waiting for that call from Martin from Highmoor, but the night passed with the telephone silent on its ebony rest. Towards dawn Kathie fell into a fitful sleep, only to be awakened by the first vague sounds of traffic in the main thoroughfare beyond the Square.

There was a feeling of relief in the fact that the new day had come at last and that some definite effort could be made to trace Shandon.

Immediately after breakfast she put a call through to Highmoor and was told in the clipped, professional tones of the night sister coming off duty that there was still no change in Miss Hamilton's condition. She tried the Penner number three times that morning, and then was forced to the reluctant conclusion that the family must be away from home. She placed the instrument back on its rest, a little frown of annoyance creasing her smooth brow. What now?

There was a small pile of letters on the desk that had come in with the morning post, and she opened them one by one. The last letter was written on thick cream note-paper and addressed in a neat hand. As Kathie read the two pages and glanced at the signature at the foot of the second a half smile played round her lips. The letter was a request from Mrs. McCallum-Blair. She would be very grateful if Miss Lang would be good enough to give her some idea of Sheena's capabilities as a dancer, and what prospects there would be of starting her on such a career!

She decided to lunch early and pay a personal call at Westwood Drive.

She ran quickly downstairs and opened the door just as the bell pealed.

It was Martin.

She noted the deep lines of fatigue round her brother's eyes, and the stern set of the usually smiling mouth.

"She's just the same. No change—nothing." He seemed to look through her, and Kathie led the way into the empty ball-room.

"Martin, you *are* telling me the truth?" she asked fearfully.

"Yes. I wish to God I could tell you something different. Have you found Shandon?"

He did not look at her as he asked the question, and Kathie felt an overwhelming rush of pity for this brother of hers who was trying to trace the one man who might put an end to all his hopes.

"I can't find anything that might help me among Arline's belongings," she explained, "and I couldn't get an answer when I 'phoned her aunt's place. I was going there now."

"I'll sit about for a bit," Martin said. "I asked the matron to 'phone me here if there was any change."

"Perhaps I should stay, too . . ."

Kathie hesitated. She was facing one of the greatest temptations of her experience. Since her mother's death nobody had mattered very much in her life except Martin; he was as dearly-beloved as a brother could be, and she was doing her best to take away the thing he prized above all else. Yet, Arline was lying there at Highmoor calling ceaselessly for this other man.

"Martin," Kathie said, "I—think I must go."

He did not turn from the window.

"I thought you had gone," he said. "Why are you waiting?"

Kathie went out with a heavy sigh. Why was life so difficult—so complicated?

When she turned into Westwood Drive, one glance at the Penner residence convinced her that the family must be out of town. The scarlet blinds were down in all the rooms, and the big main door was closed. She turned away with a sickening sense of her own inability to help Arline further. She stood at the corner of Westwood Drive, watching the ceaseless stream of traffic on the main road, and wondering what to do next.

A bus slowed down on the other side of the road to pick up a passenger. She read the name on the side window idly. Bearsden. And then, before she knew what impulse had moved her to do so, she was across the road and had boarded the bus. She could not think of anything else to do to help her friend at the moment, and she had promised Gustav to get into touch with Sheena McCallum-Blair's parents as soon as possible. She had the letter from Mrs. McCallum-Blair in her handbag. Yes, she would risk it and call at the Bearsden house.

Getting out at the station, she asked her way and was directed back along the road the bus had come. She found the house quite easily. It stood back off the main thoroughfare at the end of a long drive, and Kathie walked up between the trees, wondering what the result of her errand would be. She hoped that she could persuade Sheena's mother to let her go to London with them.

A sports car was drawn up before the glass porch, and Kathie stepped round it to the door. She pressed the bell, and stood back to wait. When a maid appeared, she asked to speak to Mrs. McCallum-Blair.

"Would you come this way?" the girl asked, showing her across the hall to a room on the left.

A man turned from one of the long bookcases which took up most of the wall space, a leather-bound volume under his arm.

"Won't you come over to the fire?" he asked, drawing forward a chair for her. "It's rather cold outside."

"Thank you."

"Had you an appointment with my mother?" he asked. "I think she must have forgotten. She went upstairs to rest after lunch."

"No, not exactly," Kathie explained. "Mrs. McCallum-Blair wrote to me about Sheena. Perhaps I had better introduce myself. I am Kay Lang."

He smiled for the first time, and held out his hand.

"I've heard more about you than about any other living creature—from Sheena," he said. "No doubt that's a brother's privilege. My name's Shandon — Gavin Shandon."

The name seemed to echo round the quiet, book-lined room until it filled it, echoing and re-echoing in Kathie's ears, and yet she stood gazing at Shandon as if she could not believe that she had heard aright. Was it possible—could it be possible?

Kathie had made decisions before on the spur of the moment and she made one now.

"Mr. Shandon," she said, "some of the things I am going to say may seem strange to you, but I am speaking from necessity—dire necessity."

"I don't think I quite understand." Shandon's voice had the suspicion of an edge to it. "Perhaps you would like to explain?"

Kathie plunged into her explanations with feverish haste.

"I'm Arline Hamilton's friend," she began, and saw his lips tighten at the mention of Arline's name. "Mr. Shandon, there's been an accident. Arline has been hurt—concussion, the doctors say—and she's calling for you. Please —no matter what has happened in the past—you'll come to her now?"

There was more than entreaty in Kathie's voice; her question was almost a command.

"Where is she?" Gavin asked, and all the grimness had suddenly gone out of his voice.

"At Highmoor Hospital." Kathie's hands were trembling now, and her voice was strangely shaken. "Will you come? Will you come at once?"

"At once," he said. "If you can wait until I explain to my mother. You can come back and see her about Sheena later."

He went quickly from the room, and Kathie wiped the sudden tears of relief from her eyes. She was standing before the fire, composed again, when the door opened and an elderly woman came in. The kindly grey eyes proclaimed her Gavin's mother.

"I had been hoping to meet you soon, Miss Lang," she said, "but not like this. We must see each other later when Gavin and you have been to—Arline." Her eyes darkened with concern for the girl at Highmoor whom she had never met. "You must go now quickly," she continued. "Every moment is precious. Good-bye, my dear, and come back again."

Kathie gripped her hands, too overwhelmed with emotion to speak, and Mrs. McCallum-Blair went with her to the car.

Shandon helped her in.

"There's just one point," he said, as they drove slowly down between the trees. "What about Arline's—fiancé? The Canadian she is going to marry?"

Kathie was silent for a moment. Then:

"She was never going to marry anyone," she replied steadily. "There has never been anyone but you."

CHAPTER ELEVEN

THE SPAN OF A RAINBOW

I

ARLINE opened her eyes and glanced round the white room where she lay. She had no trace of time. Vaguely she knew that she had been here for many days, but until this morning she had scarcely seemed to care. Shadowy figures had come and gone at her bedside and she had recognised some of them dimly as through a mist.

Her head turned restlessly on the pillow. Martin had come, Martin whom she had seen last at the wheel of the wrecked car just before it had turned over into the ditch. She shuddered, covering her eyes with her hand. She had been going to tell Martin that she would marry him, and now she knew that she could never tell him. Somehow she thought that Martin knew, too. He had told her the day before, sitting on the stiff, high-backed hospital chair beside her bed and holding her hand, that she was "out of the wood" now, and that there was no need for him to put off that sailing date any longer.

Poor Martin! The tears of weakness gathered in her eyes. He had been so kind and considerate, so infinitely patient with her. Perhaps some day he would meet someone else. . . .

There was a knock at the white door, and Kathie came in. Kathie, the same as ever, with a cheerful smile and a light word, and carrying a big sheaf of bronze chrysanthemums.

"Now, that's better!" she declared. "If you improve at this rate, we'll be able to take you home at the end of the week."

"Do you think I might?" Arline asked. "They've been kind here, Kathie, but I feel that I'm running you off your feet."

186

"Don't think about that," Kathie replied. "Concentrate on getting well. You look very much better to-day. How do you feel?"

"Much better," Arline confessed.

"Well enough to have a visitor—two visitors?" Kathie asked.

"Martin?"

"No, not this time." Kathie paused, and then went on quickly: "Mrs. McCallum-Blair and Sheena."

"But, Kathie "

"Sheena is so keen to come," Kathie said. "Gus and I have just arranged with her parents to take her to London with us, and I think she wants to tell you all about it."

"But, Kathie—Mrs. McCallum-Blair?" Arline's pale face flushed a little. "I suppose I should have told you before," she went on slowly. "She is—Gavin's mother."

"I know."

"You know? But, Kathie, how?"

"I found Gavin and brought him here."

"Kathie!" The whispered exclamation was almost a cry. "Why did you? Oh, why did you *ask* him to come?"

"Because you have been foolish long enough," Kathie said, "because people have interfered in your life in the past, and because I thought it was time someone else interfered—in a different way."

"But he could not have wanted to come," Arline protested. "It must have been because—because he was sorry for me. You see, he's in love with someone else," she ended difficultly.

"If he is, he has a queer way of showing it," Kathie declared, rising from the chair by the bedside. "Am I to bring Sheena and Mrs. McCallum-Blair to see you to-morrow?"

Arline hesitated.

"Yes," she said at last in a very small voice, "if they want to come."

She lay back among her pillows when Kathie had gone and stared up at the high white ceiling, her thoughts confused. A visit from the Mrs. McCallum-Blair she had built up in her mind would have frightened her at any other time, but just now she was too weak to care what happened.

187

The morning found her able to sit up a little, propped with cushions, and eating her first substantial meal for more than a week.

When Kathie came round the door of her room at exactly three o'clock her eyes went beyond her to the woman in grey who followed her into the room. Her heart was fluttering within her like a caged bird, but the moment she met the elder woman's kindly eyes it was as if a gentle hand had been laid on that wild fluttering, stilling it.

Sheena was at her bedside, too, a glowing, radiantly happy Sheena.

"I've wanted so much to come," she said, "and I've brought mother with me." She turned to Mrs. McCallum-Blair. "Mums, this is Arline—at last!"

Mrs. McCallum-Blair laid the jonquils she was carrying on the little side table and approached the bed.

"My dear, I *do* hope you are much better." Arline thought that she had never seen a more gentle, kindly face.

"Thank you," she murmured. "It was very kind of you to come."

There was a ridiculous lump in her throat as she thought of all she had accused this motherly woman of in her mind. If manner and appearances spoke true, Mrs. McCallum-Blair was utterly incapable of the smallest of mean actions, and Arline could not believe that she would have gossiped to Mrs. Penner about her son.

Sheena perched herself on the bed.

"I simply had to see you to tell you about my good news," she cried. "I'm to go to London to be one of Mr. Legrin's pupils, and he thinks that one day, if I work hard enough, I may be good enough for the ballet!"

Mrs. McCallum-Blair laid a grey-gloved hand on her daughter's arm.

"All right, Sheena," she agreed. "I think we may as well ask Miss Hamilton now." She turned to Arline, and her smile was infinitely tender. "We know you must rest for a little after you leave here, my dear," she continued, "and I have been suggesting to Miss Lang that you might let me offer you our little house at Winter's Quay for the purpose."

"Oh!" Tears were stinging behind Arline's eyes. "It's very good of you, but—I couldn't."

"My dear, why not? Miss Lang and you have both been very kind to Sheena and—I wish you would allow me to do this for you. It's just a very little thing in return."

Arline lay still. Something within her wanted to refuse, but she could not utter the words while these far-seeing grey eyes were looking down into her own. And yet, because they were so like Gavin's eyes, she *must* refuse.

"It's too much," she said weakly. "I can't—really accept . . ."

Mrs. McCallum-Blair bent over the bed.

"Arline—I want you to accept this offer because, you see, my dear, there are so many things that. must be straightened out just as soon as you are strong enough."

She knew! Gavin's mother knew!

Long after Mrs. McCallum-Blair had gone Arline lay with that one thought in her heart.

II

There was a rift in the grey dome of the sky, and away across the moors the clouds had parted to reveal a patch of blue which seemed more vivid to Arline than anything she could remember.

The porter was carrying her suitcase out to the car, and Arline turned to the sister.

"I want to thank you for all your kindness to me while I have been here," she said, holding out her hand. "I'm so sorry it was matron's day off. I should have liked to have said good-bye to her and thanked her, too."

The porter came back into the hall.

"Everything's ready now, miss," he said.

Arline went out through the big oak doors and found the McCallum-Blair's car pulled up in the drive. Gavin Shandon was at the wheel, and at sight of him she stopped short on the top step.

He got out and opened the door, and because, even in her first confusion, she was aware of the eyes of the sister and the porter upon her, she crossed to the big car.

"Jump in," he commanded.

She obeyed him, as she had obeyed him automatically that first day on Loch Linneh.

He let in his clutch and drove slowly down the long drive on to the moorland road.

Arline could feel her lips trembling, and her hands were clasped tightly over her bag.

"Where's Kathie?" she asked. "She promised to come for me."

He was looking straight ahead, driving slowly and carefully, because it was the first time she had been in a car since the accident, but he smiled at her question.

"Kathie's a very busy woman these days," he said. "Getting married, I'm told, is a whole-time job, so she sent a deputy. She thought that I could be trusted to bring you home as safely as she could."

There was a deep note in his voice, the note Arline remembered so well from those fleeting, happy days at Winter's Quay, when a spell had been woven in the dim heart of Puck's Wood.

"I—where are we going?"

Slowly and deliberately he brought the car to a standstill, and turned to look at her fully in the shaft of sunlight that broke through a rift in the clouds.

"My dear," he said, "I am taking you home."

With no other word spoken between them, he gathered her into the shelter of his arms, and Arline laid her head on his shoulder in a little gesture of unquestioning surrender.

When she drew away, at last, he fumbled in the pocket of his coat and produced a little leather case.

"I want you to try something on," he said, "just to make sure."

He held out his hand, and on his palm lay the plain gold circlet of a wedding ring.

"Gavin!"

"Try it," he commanded, and she slipped it on her finger and quickly off again.

"Gavin," she said, laughing a little as she met his gravely tender eyes, "how did you know the size?"

"Because of this." The three diamonds of her engagement ring flashed in his hand. "You see, perhaps it was lucky that I had it, after all."

Her eyes filled with tears.

"Can you ever forgive me for being such a fool?" she asked, her voice catching on the words. "I had no trust, I didn't stick very closely to my own ideals."

He put his arm round her and drew her close.

"We've both been fairly blind, my darling, wasting precious months because of pride and misunderstanding, but all that's over now, thank God, and we've found each other at last. We should have known that there could never have been any question of anyone else for either of us."

He bent his head, and their lips met in one long, sweet kiss, the kiss of forgiving and perfect understanding.

Presently he started the car again, and Arline said:

"You haven't told me where we are going."

He smiled down at her in his old quizzical way.

"You won't let me keep any secrets, will you?" he said. "We are going to Winter's Quay."

"Winter's Quay. Oh, Gavin!"

He laughed like a schoolboy.

"You've been there before. You'll know a little house called Rowan Gate, then? Well it's been offered to a certain Gavin Shandon on the strict condition that he gets married at once and occupies it."

"Gavin—your mother?" Arline asked, between a laugh and a sob.

He nodded.

"Yes. She's down there waiting for you now," he said. "She's helped to arrange everything, Arline, and she's quite set on a quiet wedding in the church up on the hill yonder some day—soon."

They travelled quickly along the road to the coast, and were just in time to catch a car-ferry across the Clyde. The crossing was like a dream to Arline, a strange, happy dream that was never, never going to fade.

Mrs. McCallum-Blair opened the door to them herself, and Arline passed into the warm embrace of her arms. In the hall beyond, her hand in Gustav Legrin's, Kathie stood waiting to welcome her and Sheena hopped from one foot to the other round the chief actors in the little scene.

"There's another surprise for you, Arline," Mrs. McCallum-Blair said after tea. "Sheena, what did you do with the cable?"

Sheena produced the flimsy envelope.

"It's from Martin," she cried, unable to keep the news to herself one minute longer.

The message was from Martin, sent from the boat that was taking him back to Canada, and in six words it wished them both happiness:

"All the best in the world—Martin."

When Kathie and Legrin had left for the last boat that night, and the dome of the sky was jewelled with stars, Gavin wrapped a fur-lined cloak of his mother's round Arline's shoulders, and led her out to the orchard and up to the elfin garden beneath the low stone wall.

They stood together, looking out and up to the hills above the Firth. They were clear-cut and etched darkly against the night sky and the first pale gleam of a new moon rose dimly from behind the barrier of the only cloud.

"Gavin," she said slowly, "there's always some kind of lining to every cloud, and ours has been a very beautiful one."

He held her closely to him without a word, and the peace of the garden encircled them both.

THE END